ANTEATER-BOY

A NOVEL

Dean Ammerman

KABLOONA

Eagan, Minnesota

Copyright © 2011 by Dean Ammerman

Library of Congress Control Number: 2011919058

ISBN: 978-0-9846822-0-1

First printing, November 2011

KABLOONA

www.anteater-boy.com

Cover design and art by Glorie Forliti

"A man is a hero, not because he is braver than anyone else, but because he is brave for ten minutes longer."

—RALPH WALDO EMERSON

"Superman or Green Lantern ain't got a-nothin' on me."

—DONOVAN

ANTEATER-BOY

1

Fish Eyes

"A word, Mr. Dale? A word?"

At the sound of his name, Zak Dale paused mid-step in the hallway on his way to class. The ninth grader's mind raced. The voice behind him came from Dr. Cyrus B. Fletcher, his science teacher. The tone was unmistakable: dull, rambling, insistent. The comments, too, were typical Fletcher: sentences that repeated for no reason, ended as if they were questions, and were punctuated by a sinus-clearing snort. It was definitely Dr. Fletcher.

Zak closed his eyes for an instant to ponder his future. At the same time he called up a mental picture of Dr. Fletcher. The man was middle-aged, tall, and thin, and wore wrinkled pants and floral patterned shirts. Zak took a deep breath as his mind's eye moved up from the shirt to study the features of the man's face: pale, blotchy skin scarred by acne; a nose that started out somewhat normal but ended in a large-pored point that bent toward the ground. Most remarkable, though, were the great eyes swimming in deep sockets set underneath a pair of bushy gray eyebrows. Looking into Fletcher's eyes was like looking at a fish's eyes through a magnifying glass.

All of this mental effort took a fraction of a second, after which Zak recognized the importance of talking to the teacher, pivoted on his right foot 180 degrees, and was immediately knocked to the ground by the rush of students on their way to class.

"Are you all right, Mr. Dale? Are you all right? A stampede? Most unfortunate?" said Dr. Fletcher in elliptical bursts.

Zak gathered up his books, crawled to the wall, stood up, and dusted himself off. He squinted at the teacher. The man's fish eyes seemed muddier than usual. He closed one of his own eyes. Still fuzzy. He closed his other eye. Much clearer.

"Yes, Dr. Fletcher?" Zak said, blinking wildly.

"Mr. Dale? Mr. Dale?"

"Yes? Yes?" Zak said urgently.

"Is there something wrong with your eyes, Mr. Dale?"

"What? Oh? No. No. I seem to have…that is…lost a contact?"

Whenever he talked to Dr. Fletcher, Zak Dale found himself involuntarily aping his teacher's speech, especially the way most sentences ended in a question.

"Lost a contact? Really? Where? Where?"

"On the floor, Dr. Fletcher? On the floor?"

"Yes, well, you must find it, then?" the teacher said. Dr. Fletcher made a cursory glance across the floor and then slowly raised his head and rubbed his eyebrows with an index finger. "I believe there was something…," he began. The teacher's voice drifted off and Zak was drawn away from his search for the contact lens to follow Dr. Fletcher's line of sight. It seemed directed at the sprinkler head on the ceiling where a single dusty strand of a spider web was visible in the bluish fluorescent light of the hallway.

Zak shook his head and then glanced at his watch. The watch

face was a blur. He closed one eye, then the other. He still had two minutes to get to class and no time to look for his contact lens.

"You wanted to tell me something, Dr. Fletcher?" Zak said.

"Hmm? Yes? Yes? Exactly, Mr. Dale! I am looking for someone to—how shall I say it?—clean the science laboratory this weekend. A thorough cleaning, mind you. Thorough. And I naturally thought of you, Mr. Dale. Am I right?"

"Right?"

The fish eyes bulged.

"Am I right?"

"You thought of me to clean the science lab?"

Cleaning was, at best, one of Zak's undiscovered talents. His face, hair, and clothing were always in disarray. He rarely had his notes and school assignments in order. His room was "a dump," according to his parents. Even his best friend, Miles Beakman, once suggested that he hire hazardous waste professionals to clean up after him.

Dr. Fletcher smiled broadly, showing uncommonly white, orderly teeth. "You *are* interested in the independent study project for the biology department this summer? I believe you expressed an interest?"

"Yes? I did?" Zak again shook his head to clear his thoughts. "I mean, I did. Yes." His confusion changed quickly to a vigorous nod.

Zak needed a summer job, and even if he didn't care much for biology (or for Dr. Fletcher), his lack of interest in the sciences was overmatched by a powerful interest in making money.

"I could always offer it to Miss Sather, of course," Dr. Fletcher mused. "But, naturally, I thought you would like an opportunity, since I really have little evidence at this point, to show how—that is, what—you're made of? What do you say?"

"What did you say?" Zak was momentarily befuddled, but as he ran the teacher's last few sentences through his mind, it seemed a roundabout way of asking if he wanted to clean the science lab. He did.

"I mean, yes. Of course. Yes?"

"Splendid. Then see me after school today and we can go over the particulars."

The last words barely reached Zak's ears. By then he had rejoined the river of students making their way to class.

2

Cleavage

"He wants you to clean the science lab?" Miles Beakman asked Zak in disbelief.

"That's what he said. Or what I think he said. I'm never quite sure with Fletcher." Zak quietly unwrapped and slid a cinnamon candy into his mouth. "Must be some kind of test. You know, if I do well on this he'll give me the summer job."

"Don't waste your time," Miles said. "The guy's a jerk. He's a dentist...or at least he was. That's why he expects everyone to call him 'Doctor.' Probably disbarred or something."

Miles and Zak sat at opposite ends of the farthest table in the John Quincy Adams Senior High School library. It kept them the greatest distance from the checkout desk, the computer workstations, and from the eyes and ears of Mrs. Kaufman the librarian. Flanked on one side by shelves of magazines and on the other by oversized books, the table was isolated but still gave them a view of the large, strangely-quiet room.

"I think it's worth a Saturday morning or afternoon among the test tubes and pig hearts." Zak adjusted the glasses on the bridge of his nose. He'd worn contacts so long that wearing glasses seemed foreign and uncomfortable.

"He'll have you clean the lab and turn you down for the money position," Miles said. "It's a scam. He's just looking for free work."

"I told him I'd do it. I have a meeting with him after school today."

Miles shook his head and sighed.

"Kim Sather," Zak said, thinking out loud. "She's the one I have to worry about."

"What are you talking about?"

"She's my competition for the summer job," Zak said.

"Like I said, you got no chance." Miles waved his hands dismissively. "Unlike you, Kim Sather actually *likes* science. She's good at it. She can cut up a frog, take it all apart, tell you everything that's inside, and then put it back together so it hops away happier than it was before." Miles stared at Zak. "She's also better looking than you."

"Like that matters," Zak said.

"It *always* matters."

Miles looked down at his notebook. He'd doodled in it. No words, just lines and circles. He looked up at Zak. "You start your science project yet?"

"Nah," said Zak. "Don't have a clue. You?"

"I have an idea."

"Really?" Zak pushed back from the table a little. His chair balanced on the back two legs. "You're taking this seriously?"

"I said I have an idea. That's all I said. Don't go spreading rumors, Z. I got a reputation."

"Yeah. Underachiever."

"Under *challenged*," Miles said. He added, "This could

actually be interesting."

Zak was surprised. Since elementary school, Miles had exerted as little effort as possible in class, yet when called upon he always knew the answer and always had his work done. He was a genius. That angered his classmates, frustrated his teachers, and left him without friends and supporters. Except for Zak. Zak appreciated Miles' intelligence as he did a good magic trick or the performance of a gifted athlete. And Miles was a good friend. Still, Zak had often wondered if Miles would ever truly care about anything or take himself seriously.

"What's your topic?" Zak asked.

"Junk food."

"Really?" Zak said, impressed. "Let me know if you want help with research and taste testing." He looked at his own blank notebook. "I could use a good idea, too."

At that moment Aurora Jenkins entered the library walking at high speed toward their table. As she slammed down her books and large purse, Miles and Zak jumped, and heads all across the library turned in their direction. Mrs. Kaufman gave them a menacing look.

"I have exactly three minutes," Aurora said, sliding into the empty chair at the far end of the square table. She was a round, olive-skinned girl with dark hair cut short, a smooth unmakeuped face, a small pointy nose, and intense blue eyes. She wore brown corduroy slacks, an oversized blue T-shirt, and a plaid scarf around her neck.

"Is this our daily audience with the queen?" Miles said in a low sarcastic voice.

"Shut up, Miles," Aurora snapped, then turned to Zak. "What's with the glasses?"

"Lost a contact."

9

"Again?"

Zak didn't answer.

Zak and Aurora had been in the same schools since kindergarten. They weren't exactly friends—Zak wasn't sure Aurora had any real friends—but they did talk. More accurately, Zak listened. Aurora would always arrive in a rush, make several pronouncements and one or two suggestions, condemn one or two people, add an outlandish theory or two, and then move on. All that time she would be in constant motion, vigorously chewing gum, sniffing the air for unusual smells, rubbing her fingertips together, and moving her head around like a nervous pigeon.

Zak quickly lost interest in Aurora and instead found himself staring at the librarian's desk where Mrs. Kaufman was talking to a thin, blonde-haired girl. She looked familiar. Algebra? Band? American History. That was it. Zak couldn't remember her name.

"You don't have a chance with her, you know." Aurora snapped at her gum maliciously.

Zak was startled out of his reverie and turned and blinked at Aurora.

"Mrs. Kaufman?" Miles said slyly.

"That Holmes girl," Aurora said, gesturing toward the librarian's desk. "That new hottie you and everyone else have been drooling over for the last week." Aurora dropped a quick grin onto her face and let it fall away just as fast. "Trust me, Z, you're not her type. You don't play football or basketball. You're short. You've got no musculature, no definition. You're no brain, of course, and you're not dull enough, either. If you want my honest opinion, which I'll give you, it's that you're ordinary. Maybe even a little below ordinary. It's not a bad thing, being ordinary. It's just…blah. Girls like Mia Holmes don't go for blah."

"You gonna put up with that, Z?" Miles asked, smirking.

Zak shook his head. "I don't hear it any more," he said, dismissing Aurora's ramblings. Then he squinted through his glasses at Mia Holmes. "I think she's in my history class. She's new."

"I have a bad feeling about that girl," Aurora said, leaning forward. "Look, she transfers into our school with like a month left. My guess? She was thrown out of the last school she was in. Probably expelled. Possibly on drugs. Here's what I know. Her dad has money. Drives a Mercedes. Wears fancy suits. Bought a house in the school district. Probably paid off the principal and maybe half the school board, too. This has conspiracy written all over it. I should write an article for the school paper."

"Where do you get this stuff?" Zak said.

"You can tell, can't you? I mean, just look at her. The body, the face, the smile, the hair. If I looked like that—and I'm the first one to tell you I don't, thank you very much—if I looked like that, I wouldn't be talking to you right now. No offense. I'd be in a whole other world...socially, that is."

"What world *are* you in?" Miles asked. "I mean socially, of course."

"Never you mind. I'm just here to tell you that you need to know your place."

"Our place?" Zak looked around. "We're hiding out in a corner of the library trying not to get kicked out."

"Not a bad choice, really," Aurora said, nodding approvingly. "It suits you."

Miles leaned across the table toward Aurora. "Fletcher wants Z to clean the lab on Saturday," he said. "Free. Says it's a test to see if he's the right man for the summer job."

Aurora turned to Zak. She raised an eyebrow and scoffed. "Fletcher just wants free work so he doesn't have to do it himself."

"That's what I told him," Miles said.

"I'm still doing it, no matter what you two say," Zak said.

"You're hopeless," Aurora said dismissively.

After a few seconds of silence, Miles and Zak's heads absentmindedly drifted away from Aurora and toward the librarian's desk and Mia Holmes.

"You're *both* hopeless," Aurora said, pulling a stick of gum from her purse and jamming it into her mouth.

"What?" Zak asked.

"Get over it," Aurora said. "She's new, but it won't take her long to find her place next to all the other blondies. It just makes me sick. Sick."

"You should be a ditz like that, Aurora. Life isn't fair," Miles said.

Aurora glared at Miles, smiled pitifully at Zak, turned, and left them at their isolated table, swinging her large black leather purse behind her.

Zak and Miles kept watching Mia Holmes, who was filling out paperwork or checking out a book.

"Well?" Zak asked.

"She's blonde. Natural, I think," Miles said. "Five-five or -six. Jeans. White blouse. Tennis shoes with some real wear on them. Not much makeup. Maybe lip gloss—you can see the reflection."

"Not your typical fashion princess," Zak said.

"You say she's in your history class?" Miles asked.

"I think so," Zak said uncertainly. "Things have been crazy lately. We're way behind. We just had a test on the Civil War and now we're supposed to be getting a sub."

"What's up with Ms. Jackson?"

Zak shrugged. "Don't know. I'll probably find out tomorrow."

"We're deep into World War II already," Miles said. "In fact, I

12

think I have a paper on the rise of Hitler due tomorrow."

Zak's stomach rumbled. He continued to study Mia Holmes.

"So why is it that guys like us don't end up with girls like that?" he asked.

"Speak for yourself. Nobody called *me* 'blah.'"

"Yeah, well, what's the deal?"

"It's the jungle, Z." Miles closed his book and stacked it on top of his blue spiral notebook. "In the jungle, we're, like, anteaters. You know, ugly, toothless mammals that live in South and Central America and slink around on the ground sticking their noses and sticky tongues into ant hills. We walk around like that all day with sand on our tongues looking for ants on the ground. She's different. She's a tiger or a lion, not a bug eater. Carnivore. Predator. Looks up, not down. A seriously dangerous babe."

"I don't know," Zak said. "I don't feel like an anteater."

"An *ordinary* anteater. Not even a *good-looking* anteater."

"She's not that different. She's just…a girl."

Miles leaned across the table and shook Zak's right shoulder. "Z, you have eyes. Use them."

"What are you talking about?"

Miles looked around surreptitiously, lowered his head, dropped his voice, and whispered one word: "Cleavage."

"What?"

"You heard me, anteater boy."

Zak looked again. Miles was right. When she turned their way, leaning over the desk, he could see it clearly even at that distance. Cleavage. Definite cleavage.

"I guess it's ants for lunch, huh?" Zak said.

"You got it, pal."

3

Home

The Dales lived in a small ranch-style house five blocks from the 2,200-student high school in suburban St. Paul. The well-kept, single-story 1960s home was painted celery green with broccoli-colored shutters and a brown shingled roof. It looked like a stale vegetable. A silver Honda Accord was parked in one of the stalls of the two-car garage. Indecipherable chalk drawings in white, pink, and purple covered the driveway. The lawn was more weeds than grass, and yellow patches—courtesy of their short-haired dachshund Larry—spotted the scruffy green yard like a bad case of acne.

Zak was met at the door by Larry. The boy bent down and scratched the dog's head and belly.

"Is that you, Zak?" Zak's mother, Susan Dale, called out from the kitchen. She was compact and athletic, and moved around the house in quick bursts like a bumble bee. Wisps of gray jutted out from the thin brown hair that just reached her shoulders.

"Yeah."

He came into the kitchen and set his backpack in the corner.

"How was your day at school?"

"Good."

"Anything exciting happen?"

"Not really."

Zak pulled open the refrigerator door and looked inside.

"What's that smell?" he asked, reaching in and pulling out a carton of orange juice.

"Dinner."

He poured the juice into a plastic cup, returned the carton to the refrigerator, removed two slices of bread from a bag on the counter, located the peanut butter, and made a sandwich.

"Did you have any tests today?"

"One. English. I think I did okay."

"What was it on?"

"A bunch of essays we read. Multiple choice. We had to know titles and authors and themes. You know, George Orwell. Things like that." He stuffed a quarter of the sandwich into his mouth. "I'm going over to Miles' house," he managed to say.

"Fine," his mother said. "Dinner's at six. Not six-ten. Not six-fifteen."

"I know, I know."

Zak finished his orange juice, set the cup on the counter, and opened the front door.

"I don't want to have to call you!" his mother shouted after him.

The door closed with a click.

4

The Project

Zak stepped through the front door of his home at 6:03. Virtually on time.

"Wash up. We're at the table," his mother called out.

Zak went into the bathroom and decided to use soap instead of just water, since his hands were dirty from dribbling a basketball. His feeble hand washing attempt turned the soap a dull gray, left streaks of mud in the white porcelain basin, and imprinted several dirty handprints on the beige towels. He wiped his hands on his jeans to get rid of the remaining water.

In the dining room, his mother, father, and sister Chloe were already at the dinner table. Meatloaf, potatoes, green beans, and milk stared at him.

"Not bad," Mr. Dale said, looking at his watch. "Your mother said I should call, but I said you'd be here."

"It's just a few minutes," Zak said.

Zak's parents had started a campaign to get him to be more responsible. So far it was a failure. He kept up with school, friends, reading, homework, eating, and sleeping. That was enough. The way he looked at it, there wasn't time for anything else. He was usually at home to eat dinner with his family. He felt pretty good about that.

Zak loaded his plate with large portions of everything.

"Your mother said you had a test today," Mr. Dale said to Zak.

"We had a test, too," Chloe said quickly. "In English. We had 20 words and I spelled them all right."

"Great job, honey," Mr. Dale said.

"Big whoop," Zak said.

"I don't want to hear that from you two tonight, am I clear?" Mrs. Dale said sharply.

"It wasn't me. You know it wasn't me," Chloe said.

"This time," Mr. Dale answered, glaring at Chloe.

"Just try to be nice to each other. It makes our meals so much more pleasant," Mrs. Dale said.

There was a long pause as the family concentrated on their food. The small dining room was filled with the scrape and rattle of knives and forks on plates.

"I have to be at school on Saturday morning at 9:00," Zak said, reaching for the bowl with the mashed potatoes.

"Now what did you do?" his mother asked.

"I didn't do anything," Zak said defensively. "I met with Dr. Fletcher after class today. He wants me to clean up the science lab."

"Really?" Mr. Dale asked.

"It's to see if he'll give me that job this summer."

"If you're serious about working, you should apply to a couple of other places," Mr. Dale said. "There's a lot of competition for jobs."

"What kind of summer work would it be?" Mrs. Dale asked.

"I'm not sure," Zak said. "Dr. Fletcher said something about

17

research and teeth. That's about all I know. Except that it's supposed to pay real money."

"Saturday is fine with us. Your sister has soccer that morning," his mother said. "That's where we'll be."

"We're playing Centennial," Chloe said.

"Like I care," Zak said.

"Zak."

"Will you be back in time to let Larry out? I'm not all that confident about his bladder," Mr. Dale said.

They all turned to look at Larry sitting on the floor. The dog looked up expectantly, waiting for a scrap of food.

"I suppose."

Zak took a bite of meatloaf.

"Um…I lost a contact today," Zak said.

"Another one?"

"It wasn't my fault. It popped out when I stopped to talk to Dr. Fletcher in the hall. Then I couldn't find it."

"That's three. You pay for the next one, Zak. Or it's back to the glasses for good. I mean it," Mrs. Dale said.

Zak couldn't win. It seemed like every time he had something to say it was an opportunity for his parents to criticize him. They didn't take him seriously. They asked questions, but they didn't really know what he had to go through during the day. It was like he was living in an entirely different world. He was trying to break away and get a job and money and be independent and they kept trying to pull him back or tell him that everything he was doing was wrong or bad or wouldn't help him after high school. There was never a chance to prove himself or talk about what was important to him. He always came up short.

"Chloe, what happened to you at school today?" Mr. Dale asked.

"We had somebody come in to talk about not taking drugs."

"Was it interesting?"

"I don't know."

"How can you not know?"

"I don't take drugs, so I didn't really pay attention."

Mr. Dale sighed.

"So what else is going on in school, Zak?"

"Nothing," he said. "Except I need to come up with a topic for my science project. Something that will impress Dr. Fletcher."

"You seem more and more interested in science. That's good," Mr. Dale said.

"It's not because I like it."

"What's the assignment?" Mrs. Dale asked.

"We have to write a research paper about science 'in the real world.' Like how science is changing dentistry. That was the example Fletcher used. But it could be about practically anything. He just wants us to research a topic that interests us."

"When is this due?"

"Next to last week of May. It's our final project, worth about half our grade. He's asking for volunteers to present their papers in the auditorium to all the freshman science classes, the faculty, and even some real scientists." Zak paused. "It's kind of a big deal. I'll probably have to present something to beat out Kim Sather for the summer job."

"You'll need a good topic if you want to stand out," Mr. Dale said.

"Do you have any ideas?" Mrs. Dale asked.

"I don't know. There's nothing that really interests me that much," Zak said. "Miles is doing junk food."

"I hope you apply yourself on this one," Mr. Dale said. "Both of you."

5

The Question of America

"My name is Mr. Darius Abednego Brown, and I will be your history teacher for the rest of the school year."

The room with 27 ninth graders quieted for a moment. Several students looked up at the man standing at the front of the class, a few kept their heads flat against their desks, and the rest continued talking. Darius Brown stood just over six feet tall with dark black skin and hair cut close to his scalp. He wore a tweed sport coat, khaki pants, white shirt, black shoes, and a black belt.

"Who are you?" Bobby Preston asked lazily.

"I have already made my introductions," Mr. Brown said in a louder voice. "But, as is often the case with history, I will repeat myself." He paused and looked over the class, which gradually quieted. "As I said before, I am Mr. Brown, your new history teacher."

"What happened to Ms. Jackson?" Candice Daniels said.

"She is unable to complete her term."

"I heard she has cancer," Katie Ramerez said.

"I'm sorry, I do not know anything about Ms. Jackson. We

have never met and never spoken."

"Lucky you," Maggie Cho said, snapping her gum.

"I heard she has to get a new kidney. Remember how pale she looked?" Tom Gleason said.

"I was hired by your principal to take over Ms. Jackson's responsibilities teaching history." Darius Brown looked around the classroom. "For the remainder of the year, we will be talking about the American Revolution."

"We already did that months ago. We're almost onto World War I," said Beth Sanders helpfully.

"Over the course of the next month and a half—your final weeks as students of the ninth grade—I will do my best to learn your names. At the same time, I hope you will do your best to learn your American history. Are we in agreement?"

"Sure," said Bobby Preston smugly.

The class laughed.

"And your name is…?" Mr. Brown asked Bobby Preston, who was slouching in his chair.

"Bob," he said. "I'm Bob Preston. But they call me Fuzz 'cause of my beard." He massaged his chin where a few fuzzy hairs poked through the skin.

"Mr. Fuzz, what can you tell me about the American Revolution?"

"It happened in America," he said.

The class laughed.

"That's a start," Mr. Brown said.

A large girl with black hair raised her hand and started speaking. "I'm Martee Freeman, Mr. Brown, and, like Beth said, we're already past the American Revolution. In fact, we're past the Civil War and Reconstruction. Ms. Jackson told me she was getting ready to start with World War I. She already had some

DVDs picked out. We watch a lot of DVDs."

"Thank you, Miss Freeman," Mr. Brown said.

"You're welcome."

"You may have been anticipating a spirited discussion of the events that led up to the first world war, but instead we will spend this last month reviewing the American Revolution."

"Are we going to, like, learn about Martin Luther King, Jr.?" Candice Daniels asked.

"Tell me, Miss…"

"Daniels."

"Miss Daniels. Tell me, was Dr. King involved in the American Revolution?"

"No. But he was, like, a famous…person."

"During the American Revolution?"

"No."

"We will be talking about the American Revolution."

"But you're black."

"Yes. You are correct. I am black."

"And Martin Luther King, Jr., he was black and really important."

"If I remember my history, Dr. King was black. That is right. Still, as significant a man as he was, he was not a key figure in the American Revolution."

"How come?" Jason Wiley asked.

Darius Brown stood and looked at the class, trying to make eye contact with each student. Suddenly his mouth formed a broad smile.

"Like yourselves, Dr. King was not alive during the American Revolution. Like yourselves, Dr. King was profoundly affected by the events that took place from the 1760s to the end of the 18th century."

"So…," Fuzz Preston began.

"So it is time for me to ask the questions."

Zak listened to the buzz of conversation around him. Nothing registered. He kept looking toward the front of the room where Mia Holmes sat. He watched as she listened to the new teacher with her notebook open and pen ready. The fact that she used a pen rather than a pencil surprised him. People who use pens are confident, sure of themselves, he thought. Zak looked down at the stub of a #2 pencil in his own hand. Then he looked up at the new teacher. Mr. Bowen? Mr. Braun? Mr. Brine? Mr. Brown. Brown. Memorizing names and dates gave him trouble, which was why he was lucky to have managed a low C in American History so far. He was sure he failed his last test. Ms. Jackson's tests were all about famous people—when they were born, when they died, when a certain battle happened. She showed movies and TV shows with images of maps and paintings and dead people. None of it ever seemed real to him. The names and dates became a jumble in his mind. Once, in a panic, he even misspelled his own name on a test. It was a disaster. His only bit of luck was that he had a seat directly behind Jeremiah Koll, the six-foot two-inch offensive lineman for the football team. Zak was completely hidden from view and never had to answer any questions. But Jeremiah was at the doctor's office with a sprained knee, leaving a single empty desk and an unobstructed view of Zak. He felt like a target. As the new teacher moved away from the whiteboard and toward the class, Zak slid lower in his chair.

"The question I want you to consider is this: why is the American Revolution so important?" Mr. Brown asked.

"It's the start of our country," Nicole Anderson said.

Zak smirked. Nicole had an answer for everything.

"Yes. But why does that matter?"

"It's the start of democracy," Randy Caton said.

Zak looked over at Randy Caton. He was annoying. He liked to hear himself talk.

"Was the American Revolution about democracy?" Mr. Brown asked.

"Freedom. It was about freedom," Betty Ng said excitedly.

Zak had known Betty for years and the Ngs were friends of his parents. Betty was okay.

"Yes. That's right. But there's more to it." The class was silent. Darius Brown's eyes scanned the class. All 28 minus one. Why did Jeremiah have to pick today to go to the doctor, Zak wondered. He slouched even more, looked down at his stubby pencil, and repeated quietly to himself, "Not me, not me, not me."

"Mr. …in the blue T-shirt."

Zak looked up. Why did he have to wear a blue T-shirt today of all days? He had been thinking about the red one with Astro Boy. Or the black one with the TARDIS.

"Yes. Tell me, Mr. …."

The teacher was looking right at him. There was no escape.

"Dale." Zak gulped his own name. It came out like the sound of a frog.

"Mr. Dale. Thank you. Why do you think the American Revolution is so important?"

"Um…I don't know," Zak said. He felt like the world was staring at him.

"I know. This is not an easy question. But put yourself in the position of someone who lived back then. No cars. No computers. No electric guitars. When America—what there was of it—was ruled by Great Britain, the most powerful nation in the world. Freedom is close, but not quite right."

The teacher stared. There was a long pause. Zak saw Mia

24

Holmes looking at him. He had to say something.

"Um," Zak began. "I guess, maybe, it's about who we are. Or, maybe, who we want to be. I mean, not being controlled by anybody else."

Zak scrunched his eyes and looked down and then up. Waiting. Waiting to be told that he was wrong and stupid and didn't understand history. Waiting to be put in his place. Waiting for the C minus to be branded on his forehead.

Instead, he was greeted with thunder. "Exactly!" the teacher's voice boomed.

Darius Brown turned and pounded his fist on the metal desk at the front of the classroom, then he turned back to face the class. "Mr. Dale, you have that exactly right. The American Revolution is about who we are and who we want to be. It's about our identity. It's about a chance to become something different. Deciding our own fate. Who did they want to be? Who do you want to be? That is why I am taking us back to the American Revolution. Over the next few weeks we will answer the question of America itself."

6

The Elements

Zak unzipped his backpack, pulled out a battered textbook, a crumpled notebook, and several worksheets, and spread them across the living room floor. He turned on the TV, stuck an earbud in each ear to listen to music, set out a freshly popped bag of popcorn, and opened his science book. Friday night was early to be studying, but he wasn't sure how long it would take him to clean the science room on Saturday, and Sunday he had to go to church and then visit his grandmother. There was no telling when he'd get back, and he had no idea how he was going to find any time to learn the elements. Larry the dachshund sat close by, his intent, hopeful eyes moving from Zak to the popcorn bag and back.

The universe was made out of elements. He knew that. But only a limited number of elements. Fletcher had said something about elements in class. Years ago someone put together a chart of all those elements. Zak moved his finger down a paragraph in his textbook to a name in bold: Dmitri Mendeleev. Then he looked at the periodic table of the elements on the next page. Everything in the universe is on this one chart, he thought. That was pretty amazing. It didn't matter if it was a llama, a rock, an ice cube, or a chocolate bar. If it was in the universe, the stuff it was made of was on the chart. That was interesting. Trouble was, nothing on the chart made sense. It was in some kind of code: Ti, Nb, Re, Pb, Eu, and more. Zak pulled out a handful of popcorn, tossed a few popped kernels to the dog, ate the rest, and looked over the assignment sheet.

"You will need to know the names and abbreviations of the elements in the periodic table of the elements," it said.

Zak looked at Larry. The dachshund looked back. "This is not good," Zak said out loud.

Larry licked his lips.

"Maybe there's a trick to it," Zak said. He spotted his lucky number, 33, next to As and looked it up in the textbook. "As. Arsenic." Zak shook his head. "Maybe I'm supposed to poison myself."

Zak looked up another element. La. Larry or Louisiana? Nope. Lanthanum.

He closed the book and put in a DVD of one of his favorite old black and white movies: "The Mark of Zorro." Lanthanum? What was made out of Lanthanum? He dug his cell phone out of his pocket and called Miles.

"Yeah?"

"You know anything about Lanthanum?"

"What's up?"

"I need to memorize the periodic table," Zak said. "It doesn't make sense."

"We went through that earlier this year. It's a beautiful thing."

"Yeah, well, you're in Advanced Chemistry."

"That doesn't mean anything." There was a pause. "I'm

coming over."

Miles lived with his mother about three blocks away from the Dale house. His parents had divorced when Miles was three. His father lived in Texas with a new wife and three kids. Miles hadn't seen his father in more than a year, although they talked over the phone on the major holidays. He had no brothers or sisters, and since his mother worked long hours selling real estate he was often alone.

It took Miles about six minutes to get to Zak's house.

"Where is everybody?" he asked.

"Some soccer meeting, I guess," Zak said.

Larry waddled over and looked up at Miles.

"Hey, Lar. What's up?"

The brown dachshund wagged his tail and Miles bent over and scratched the top of the dog's head.

Zak handed Miles a Coke and they walked out to the family room, Larry trotting closely behind.

"Zorro again?" Miles said, staring at the black and white images on the TV screen.

"It's a classic," Zak said. "Tyrone Power and Basil Rathbone, good against evil."

"I'm not into all that sword fighting and horses and stuff," Miles said.

"Zorro is like a superhero," Zak said excitedly. "Wears a mask. Fights the bad guys. Gets the girl."

"And brands his enemies with a Z," Miles said, moving his wrist back and forth as if he held a foil.

"I'd rather watch the movie than do homework," Zak said.

"You have plenty of time," Miles said, sitting on the floor and picking up Zak's science book. "It's only Friday. What do you have to know…the atomic numbers, weights, and melting points?"

"No, it's matching. I just gotta match the element with its letters on the chart."

"You can do that, Z. No problem."

"Miles, you know I stink at memorizing."

"It's not that bad," Miles said. He looked at the TV and then back at Zak. "Tell me, Z, what was Daredevil's secret identity?"

"Matt Murdock. Lawyer."

"Who was the sixth Doctor?"

"Colin Baker."

"Who wrote *VALIS*?"

"Philip K. Dick."

"Leader of the Kinks?"

"Ray Davies."

"Zorro?"

"Don Diego de Vega."

Miles paused, stared at Zak, and then said, "Do you get my point?"

Zak was unconvinced. "Yeah, yeah. But this is different, Miles."

"Your memory is fine. It's just the way your brain works," Miles said. "Once you figure it out, it'll be easy."

"Oh, yeah? Look at this. Number 79. Au? It's gold. That just doesn't make sense."

"Yeah, well, aurum is the word for gold in Latin."

Zak sighed. Everything came so easily to Miles. It was frustrating. Miles knew the speed of a hummingbird's wings. He knew the name of the actor who played the first Tarzan. He knew Babe Ruth's batting average in 1923. Weird things. What surprised Zak was that he was always there to help him out. Miles didn't talk down or make fun of him or look for other friends. Zak asked him about that once, and Miles said it was because in second grade Zak gave him a piece of petrified wood. Zak didn't remember, but Miles did. He never forgot anything.

"All you need is some kind of memory trick," Miles said. "Think about this. They have gold in Australia, right? Au for Australia. See what I mean?"

"They have gold in lots of other places. Fort Knox, China, Germany…"

"That's not the point. All you have to remember is that they have gold in Australia. You see Au and what do you think of? Australia. And when you think of Australia?"

"Gold," Zak said.

"Exactly."

Zak sat for a moment thinking about the way his brain worked. He could never remember facts without some context. And for names—real people—he needed a face or something real to go along with it. His only hope was to trick himself into remembering the elements. Miles was right.

"This might work," Zak said.

"Of course it'll work," Miles said. "I mean, some of it's easy." He pointed to the periodic table in the book. "H for hydrogen. Remember the Hindenburg that blew up? The big zeppelin? It had hydrogen in it. H is hydrogen and Hindenburg."

Zak laughed. "Sounds like a kid's book. H is for hydrogen."

"That's the idea. It's that easy."

"Okay. H is hydrogen. Got it."

"He is for helium. When you breathe it in, helium makes your voice all funny, right? And that makes you laugh. He he he he. Get it? That Russian guy who came up with this chart had a real sense of humor. Probably played around with helium at parties. A real cut-up."

"He for helium. So far so good," Zak said. "Boron. Carbon.

30

Nitrogen. O for oxygen. Ne for Neon. You're right. I can do this. I just panicked." Zak looked more closely at the chart and scratched his head. "What's that Li?"

"Lithium. It's used in batteries and grease and stuff."

"So…batteries lie?"

"Let me think."

Miles tilted his head back and looked around the room. Loose clumps of dust and dog hair hid in the corners. Tyrone Power was swashbuckling on mute. Larry inched toward the bag of popcorn.

"Try this: it comes from Lithuania."

"What?"

"You know, Lithuania. The country. A lot of these elements end with 'ium.' You got helium. 'He' and 'ium.' Helium. When you get stuck, just add an 'ium' on the end.

"Lithuanium."

"Works for me."

"I thought this was science, not geography."

"Check out 98."

"Cf…Californium?" Miles smiled and Zak shook his head. "What's next, New York-ium? Texas-ium? Minnesota-ium"

"Be for beryllium."

"That's trouble."

"Be real, man."

Z laughed.

"Be real-ium."

"You got it," Miles said.

7

Sheep Brain

"Right on time, Mr. Dale?"

Zak checked his watch and saw that it was three minutes before nine on Saturday morning. He looked up and smiled weakly at Dr. Fletcher, who stood in front of the door to the science room.

"I'm pretty punctual," Zak said, trying to put on a good face but knowing that it was stretching the truth. He was punctual with his friends and usually managed to get to class on time, but other than that he was routinely late. His mother always said it started from the day he was born: ten days past his due date. They had to induce labor. "Otherwise," his mother said, "you'd still be in there."

Dr. Fletcher unlocked the door, flipped the light switch, and led Zak inside. Even though Zak had Chemistry every school day, it was as if he saw the classroom for the first time. It was a mess. Books and papers were piled in the corners; dust blanketed almost every surface; bottles and test tubes and flasks sat in sinks or in messy crowds on tables; scales and weights were bunched together like a train wreck; a pile of igneous, metamorphic, and sedimentary rocks sat in a couple of distressed boxes on a dirty table; a stuffed armadillo named Felix was fixed to a wooden stand and stared back at him; bags of garbage took up a corner of the room next to the four filthy windows; overflowing buckets of kitty litter sat in the front of the room near the whiteboard, which was covered with words and formulas in several colors; long-necked faucets that were dull and crusted with white chemical deposits dripped irregularly; the sinks at the eight individual workstations were filled with more glassware; a five-year-old computer and monitor leaned precariously against one wall; Bunsen burners were in a jumble on two shelves; a large, distressed, yellowing periodic table of the elements hung at an angle on the wall; and dozens of glass containers filled with cow eyeballs, sheep brains, fetal pigs, pig hearts, and unidentified animal parts floating in murky yellow liquids were shoved into a corner on a high shelf.

"Needs a little tidying up, don't you think?" Dr. Fletcher said encouragingly. "But I trust you can make it shine like new. Am I right?"

"Sure. Um…what do you want me to do?" Zak asked.

"Clean the test tubes, beakers, and flasks, and put them in that cabinet over there, I think," Dr. Fletcher said. He gestured toward some unknown area on the right side of the room. "Organize the books and papers and put them over there." Dr. Fletcher gestured to another undefined area of the classroom. "Everything in its place? Spick-and-span?" The teacher took a step into the room and straightened a chair with an attached desk. He stood back, looked critically at the chair, then straightened it again. "Yes," he said, nodding. "Dust and straighten everything, of course. You will find detergent, soap, and cleaning rags and brushes in one of the cabinets." Again, a feeble gesture that seemed unrelated to an object or location.

"How much time do I have?" Zak asked quietly, numbed by the task ahead of him. He glanced at the round clock on the wall.

"Whatever it takes, I think?" Dr. Fletcher edged toward the door. "I will not be back today, but I will come in early Monday morning to check on your work. Yes?"

"Yes?"

"Everything will be ready, Mr. Dale?"

"Yeah. Sure," he said. "Spick-and-span?" He added a smile of his own.

"Excellent. Excellent," the science teacher said with a toothy grin. "I knew I could trust you with this responsibility. Just lock the door when you finish and I will see you in class on Monday."

Dr. Fletcher rose on the tips of his feet, took a breath, opened his eyes wide, and tugged at his vest. Then he walked out of the classroom.

Zak turned to look at the door. He closed his eyes and muttered a curse. Two curses. He opened his eyes and cursed again. He found his regular seat—second row, third from the wall—sat down and looked around. It was overwhelming. He needed a strategy. He thought about his own room and what his mother always said: "Zak, start with the obvious." In his own room he could never figure out what was obvious, so he pretty much left everything as it was. Here it was a little easier. Several bags of garbage leaned in a corner by the windows. He got up, grabbed two of the bags, and took them out to the dumpster in the back of the building next to the parking lot, using Felix to prop open the steel exit door. He dragged a few more bags out. It was a good start. He nodded approvingly. What next?

Since he didn't know where anything was or where anything went, he opened every drawer in every workstation and every cabinet. That was a mistake. Most contained more dusty glassware, books, and papers.

"I should've listened to Miles and Aurora," Zak said to himself.

Zak stood around for a few minutes waiting for a miracle to happen; then he got to work. He pulled all the glassware out and put it on a back table. He located the cleaning supplies, which looked as though they had never been used, filled one of the sinks with soapy water, and started washing. After more than an hour of washing and rinsing, he wiped the insides of the cabinets and carefully replaced the glassware.

At about 10:30 he heard activity in other parts of the school building. Noise and music and laughter. Some kind of concert, game, or sport, he suspected. Zak never participated in any school activities. It was one of his abiding principles: be invisible. He quit piano in the fourth grade. He never joined choir because he couldn't sing on key. His French horn playing was terrible and he only took Band for the credit. He played soccer for a couple of years, but because of his lack of size and speed he dropped to lesser and lesser teams until he wasn't on a team at all. Zak liked shooting baskets but hated organized sports. He had no interest in athletics or the school newspaper, chess club, debate, or any of the dozens of other approved school activities.

He kept working. He cleaned the tables, chairs, and workstations; threw away papers and tests that were two or three years old; grouped all the textbooks together and stacked the other books with titles like *The Fundamentals of Anatomy*, *Biology Basics*, *101 Chemical Experiments*, and *Advanced Oral Hygiene*; discarded bent and broken models of DNA strands made from Styrofoam; dusted and straightened the periodic table of the elements; cleaned the windows and heat registers; removed wads of gum from the bottoms of tables and chairs (including some he'd put there himself); consolidated the kitty litter into labeled containers with lids; and placed a cleaned and polished Felix on the high shelf at the back of the room so it could watch over the room like the patron saint of science.

Zak surprised himself. The room was transformed. It looked clean, neat, and organized, and even smelled lemon-fresh thanks to the scent of the cleaning liquid. He smiled. All that remained was a quick sweep of the floor and to arrange the jars of animal parts on the high shelf near the armadillo. He checked the clock: just past 11:30. Plenty of time to get home, take Larry outside, and hang out with Miles.

Zak moved a chair to the back of the room, stepped onto the seat and then onto the countertop, and wiped the mysterious glass containers with a damp cloth. He peered closely at the cow eye, which looked sightlessly back at him. He placed the jar neatly on the top shelf with the label forward. It looked good. Next to that he added the jars with the fetal pig, pig heart, crayfish, starfish, frog, and three other preserved specimens. Then he lowered himself to the floor and held up the last of the containers. It was labeled "Sheep Brain." Zak held it up to the light. What does a sheep think about, he wondered. Does it think about the meaning of life? What's the meaning of life to a sheep? Suspended in the murky liquid, the brain looked like a pale and lifeless sea creature with Medusa-like coils. Disconnected pieces of tissue orbited the soggy organ.

As Zak stood on the chair and prepared to place the bottled brain on the shelf, the glass jar slid out of his hands and shattered on the floor. It was an explosion. Shards of glass flew everywhere. In the center of the floor the sheep brain lay in a translucent, gelatinous puddle against a chair leg.

Zak was frozen in place and his eyes teared from the

formaldehyde vapors.

He swore. Then swore again and again and again. Loudly.

Zak didn't know what to do. He looked at the clock, then stared at the periodic table of the elements. H…hydrogen. He… helium. Li…what story could he make up to tell Fletcher? Be… be real, be strong. B. Don't "B" a moron. Boron. C…carbon. If he had a car he could drive away and leave everything behind. N is for nitrogen and nit wit and nincompoop. What a stupid thing to drop that glass. O…oxygen…breathe. F. Yeah, Fffffff…fluorine. Fluorine. That said it all.

"Hello? Is something wrong?"

Zak was jarred from his despair by someone at the classroom door. As he looked closely he recognized the face and the body: blonde hair, black turtleneck, blue jeans, and running shoes. Mia Holmes. Those fumes must really be screwing with my head, he thought. As she walked into the room and set down a small black purse, Z shook his head vigorously.

"Something really stinks in here," she said. "Are you okay?"

"Yeah," he said. "I mean, not really. I just broke something." He struggled with the words, which sounded like, "Ijabrosthing." But as she approached, Zak clearly shouted out, "Stop!" She stopped. "There's glass. And a brain. On the floor. There." He pointed.

"A brain on the floor?" she asked, confused.

"Sheep brain. It's what was in the jar that broke."

"I was out helping with the prom posters and I heard a crash," she said, gesturing toward the door. "Do you need some help?"

Zak couldn't believe what was happening. He knew this was a disaster and that Fletcher would probably kill him, but at the same time he was excited to be talking to Mia Holmes. She seemed like a nice, normal person, and not a witch or a ditz like Aurora had said.

"Sure," he said. "But be careful. And the smell is terrible. It's probably deadly."

Zak lowered himself from the chair, finding a clear spot where the floor wasn't covered with glass or liquid or brain. As he did that, Mia Holmes brought over one of the containers of kitty litter.

"Do you know where there's a dustpan and broom?"

"Up by the front desk. In that cabinet next to the computer," Zak said. "I'll open the windows so we can breathe." Zak opened three of the windows, letting in the cool, clean air.

"That smell is awful," Mia said, opening the cabinet door and removing the cleaning tools. "What happened?"

"Dr. Fletcher asked me to clean the room. I was almost done and as I was putting the jar with the sheep brain up on the shelf, it slipped. It was just dumb."

Mia Holmes came closer to where Zak was standing.

"That the brain?" she said, pointing to the gray mass on the floor.

Zak nodded.

"We can put down the kitty litter and scoop it all into a garbage bag," she said confidently.

"That's a great idea," Zak said. "I'll just clear away some of the chairs and stuff, and maybe pick up some of the big pieces of glass."

"Don't cut yourself," Mia said.

Zak opened a drawer and pulled out a black garbage bag, then bent down and picked up three large glass shards, and gently placed them in the bottom of the bag.

"I don't think I introduced myself. I'm Mia Holmes. I'm new here."

"I'm Zak. Zak Dale. But everybody calls me Z."

"Z," she said. "I like that." Mia seemed genuinely pleased to get to know Zak. Zak still felt nervous.

"You don't have to help, you know," Zak said to Mia. "It's probably dangerous."

"I'd like to help," she said. "I was just finishing up when I heard the crash and," she looked up at Zak, "and lots of swearing."

"Sorry."

"It's okay. I would have reacted the same way."

Together they spread the kitty litter over the foul-smelling liquid and the brain, and started sweeping toward the center of the spill.

"It's pretty gross," she said. "I wonder why they even have something like this here."

"Make it look like an official science room, I suppose," Zak said. He pointed up toward Felix and the remaining glass jars. "There are cow eyeballs and unborn pigs up there, too."

"A sheep brain," Mia Holmes said, sweeping closer to the center of the spill. "I wonder what a sheep thinks about."

"I thought that same exact thing," Zak said enthusiastically.

Mia Holmes looked around the classroom and then at Zak. "I noticed you in American History. Mr. Brown got all excited when you answered his question yesterday."

Zak was amazed. Because Mia Holmes was new to the school, she didn't know he was a C minus. She didn't know he was "blah." She even thought he was good at American history. It was like he was a normal human being and not an anteater.

"If you can hold open the bag, I'll fill it up and take it out to the dumpster," Zak said.

"We should put it in a box so it doesn't break open and make a big mess."

"Good idea. There's a box by the door." Zak got the box and

placed the garbage bag inside. "And I'll let the janitor know. I don't think he'll turn me in."

Once they put the brain, kitty litter, and glass into the bag, Zak tied it shut, closed the box flaps, and took the container out to the back of the school and set it beside the dumpster. He walked slowly back to the science classroom expecting it to be empty, but Mia Holmes was still there. His heart beat a little faster.

"I can still smell it," Zak said, crossing the room to close the windows. "The formaldehyde, I mean."

"I have an idea," Mia said.

She went to her purse and took out a small, round, orange bottle and emptied it onto the spill area. A wave of orange-scented perfume almost knocked him over.

"It's called Citronesia. It's a wonderful scent, but I have to be careful because it's so strong."

"Thanks," Zak said shyly, choking on the intense perfume that hung like an invisible cloud.

"Happy to help." Mia coughed and looked around the science classroom. "It looks nice. You did a good job."

"I don't know. Dr. Fletcher's going to notice something's wrong."

"What do you mean?"

"The missing brain."

"You think so?"

"I'm sure of it," Zak said. "He seems to notice everything that's not important."

"Does he do anything with them?" She pointed to the jars on the top shelf. "Are they part of his classes or research or anything?"

"No. They just sit there. You should have seen the dust. It was ugly."

"What if," Mia Holmes' voice suddenly became quieter,

"what if we put a different brain up there?"

"I think I saw this in 'Frankenstein,'" Zak said. "Like a criminal sheep's brain?"

Mia Holmes laughed.

"It doesn't have to be a brain at all," she said. "Can you find another jar like the one you broke?"

"Sure. There are a couple in the center cabinet. I washed them this morning."

Zak looked at the clock. It was 12:37.

"Now all we need is a spare brain."

8

Golden Meadows

"Are you sure this is okay?" Zak asked.

Zak and Mia walked side by side along a concrete sidewalk lined with maple trees and green grass. Zak cradled the empty glass container and lid in his hands.

"My house makes the most sense," Mia said. "We're still unpacking, but my mom will be happy I'm meeting people and not sitting around watching TV or on my phone."

Zak looked over at Mia and noticed they were about the same height. At five-feet four-inches, he was shorter than most of the students in the school.

"Um...where did you come from?" Zak asked. "I mean, I mean, where did you live before this?"

"Outside Wausau. Central Wisconsin."

They walked past the entrances to two suburban developments—Willowgate and Northbrook—down a hill and past a hedge of lilac bushes. Zak had to work to keep up.

"Do you miss it?"

"The school? Yeah...well, no, not really. It's like, there's all these different cliques and you have to do what everybody wants to do and wear what everybody wears. You can't be yourself."

Zak shrugged. "It's the same here," he said. "Probably the same everywhere."

"You try to fit in."

"I can't see you having trouble getting friends, though," Zak said.

"What do you mean?"

"I don't know. It's like you're real easy to talk to and everything."

"It's hard to get to know people. That's why I was helping with the posters."

She stopped and looked at Zak.

"It's not easy to fit in," Mia said. "If you're new, it's like people look at you and they think they know everything about you. Where you belong. You know what I mean? I almost dyed my hair before I came here. I didn't want to be another blonde. I wanted to be...someone else." She looked at Zak and started walking again. "Boys don't know what it's like."

"I think everybody wants to be someone else," Zak said.

"I'm really not what people think," she said. "My teeth are crooked." Mia bared her teeth. They were small and white and looked straight to Zak. "I've got all these zits. You can't see them because I use concealer on them." She pointed to her cheeks and forehead. Zak squinted but saw only a few small, red blemishes. "And my feet. I have to wear orthotics in my shoes." She lifted her left running shoe and wiggled it.

"I never noticed any of that."

"That's nice of you to say," she said and smiled. "What about you?"

"Me? I guess my feet are okay."

"I mean, what's your group?"

Zak laughed. "You're looking at it."

"You must have friends."

"Sure," Zak said. "There's my best friend, Miles Beakman. He's cool. And there's others I hang with sometimes, but mostly it's just me and Miles."

"That's sad," she said quietly.

Zak thought about that. He had one good friend he could count on. Was that sad?

"I don't know," he said. "I don't need that many friends."

"You're going to want lots of friends when you're old. My grandma told me that," Mia said. "Here. You can add me to your phone." She pulled her phone from the side pocket of her purse and waited as Zak managed to get his ancient, pathetic-looking phone from his back pocket. They exchanged numbers. "Now you have one more friend." She wore a self-satisfied smile as if she had just saved Zak from homelessness.

"Thanks," Zak said. He'd never had a girl's phone number before.

They turned into a new housing development with a sign that said "Golden Meadows." Zak saw large two-story homes with three-car garages, a few empty lots, two houses under construction, small trees planted in the middle of newly-sodded lawns, and a small pond.

"We're still moving in so it's really a mess," Mia said. "Like I said, everything's in boxes."

Mia led Zak up to the front of a large home with a forest green door, forest green shutters, and white siding. It was twice the size of Zak's house. Mia opened the front door and led Zak through a maze of boxes in the entryway, past a stairway, and into a kitchen filled with even more boxes.

"Mom?" Mia called out.

Mia looked around and poked her head through two nearby doorways.

"Are you done already, honey?" a voice said. A silver-haired woman walked out from behind some boxes marked "Kitchen" and gave Mia a hug. She wore a white apron and yellow rubber gloves, and held a dripping pink sponge in her right hand. Zak jumped back, startled, and nearly dropped the glass container.

"You're just in time to help clean the cupboards. I can't believe the amount of dust and sawdust in the cabinets. We should probably bring the builder back and have him clean them himself." She turned from Mia to look at Zak and then back at Mia. "Who's your little friend?"

Zak winced.

"Mom, this is Z. I met him today at school."

"I see. You're part of the prom decorating group?" she asked Zak.

"Not exactly."

"He was working…cleaning the science room," Mia said.

"Maybe you can help here," Mrs. Holmes said. She had an attractive face, with high cheekbones, full lips, and a nose that turned up slightly. He could see Mia's face in her mother.

"I can…if you want," Zak said. He looked at Mia.

"Z was cleaning the science room and accidentally dropped a sheep brain on the floor. We need to find a substitute brain to put back before the teacher finds out, so that's why we're here."

"Well, we don't have any sheep, I'm afraid," Mrs. Holmes said, smiling. "But you can use whatever we do have."

Zak set the glass container on an empty space on the kitchen table.

"We just need something that'll look like a brain in

45

formaldehyde," Mia said.

"That would be tonight's dinner," Mrs. Holmes said.

They all laughed.

"I need to finish unpacking," Mrs. Holmes said, opening a box and staring at the contents. "You'll figure something out."

"Thank you," Zak said. "This is really nice of you."

Mia and Zak both began to look around and then faced each other.

"I don't know where to start," Zak said.

"Maybe Jell-O," Mia said. "We could mix some different flavors together to get the right color, and make a mold out of something so it looks like a brain."

"It would just dissolve, wouldn't it?" Zak asked. "I mean, it's going to be at room temperature."

"Clay?" Mia suggested. "No. It's too heavy. It would just sink to the bottom of the jar. Unless we used honey. It wouldn't move around in that."

"I don't know. I think we need something a little more runny to match what's in the other jars," Zak said. "Like...cooking oil, maybe."

"Do you remember what the brain looked like? I mean, I just saw it on the floor."

"Not exactly," Zak said, thinking, remembering. "It was kind of gray. And there were these things like Styrofoam peanuts that kind of stuck out."

"Let's see. Pasta. Rice. Couscous. Chicken. Mashed potatoes."

"Mashed potatoes might work," Zak said.

"They might break up sitting in the oil, though."

Zak pictured the sheep brain and tried to think of something that would have the same look inside the glass container.

"Marshmallows," he said.

"What did you say?" Mia asked.

"Nothing," Zak said. "I was just thinking. All that wrinkly stuff on the side of the brain reminds me of marshmallows."

Mia went to the kitchen counter and picked up a paring knife. The sunlight through the window made it glow, almost like it was on fire. She slit open the packing tape on three boxes, looked inside, and shook her head.

"Mom," Mia said loudly, "do we have any marshmallows?"

Mrs. Holmes suddenly appeared from among the cartons, set a box on the counter, and looked through it quickly. Then she opened another box and another until at last she exclaimed, "Aha!"

The marshmallow bag was sad-looking. The colorful plastic package was wrinkled and worn, and the mini-marshmallows inside were pressed into dry clumps.

Mia cut open the bag, took out a handful of marshmallows, and gave them to Zak.

"What do you think?" she said.

"It could work," Zak said, squeezing the spongy pieces together. "Maybe we could heat them up in the microwave so they'll stick together."

"They're not exactly the right color," Mia said.

"We could roll them on the floor. That way they'll pick up some dust," Zak said.

Zak and Mia each squeezed a handful of marshmallows into a ball, then they rolled the balls across the kitchen floor. They compared the results. Bits of dust, dirt, sawdust, and hair clung to the white and gray pieces.

"They're disgusting," Mia said, smiling.

Zak smiled back. "Perfect," he said.

"So now we just nuke them," Mia said.

"Let's put the two together so we have left and right sides,"

Zak said.

Zak took Mia's dirty marshmallow ball and squeezed his and hers together to form a single brain.

"I didn't think science could be this much fun," Zak said.

Mia put the fuzzy glob of marshmallow on a plate and set the microwave timer on high. They watched as the brain started to bubble and move like a creature coming to life. When it started crackling and steaming they turned off the oven and took out the plate.

"It's amazing," Zak said.

"Looks almost like a real brain," Mia said. "With a little lint."

Zak picked it up. It was hot but malleable. He smoothed some of the lumpy sides, shaped it more like a brain, and pushed it inside the glass container. It fit perfectly.

"Now all we need is to add the oil, attach a label, and we're done," Zak said.

"Do you know how you'll get it back into the science room?"

Zak thought for a second. The brain had to be put in place before Dr. Fletcher noticed. The school was probably closed, and it wouldn't be open until Monday morning when the teacher returned. Besides, he had locked the room to make sure no other damage was done. They'd have to be there early to make the switch.

Zak looked at Mia. "We need it first thing Monday morning, I think," he said.

Mia nodded.

"Mom, do we have any cooking oil?" Mia asked a stack of boxes.

"The only cooking oil I have is extra virgin olive oil from Italy," Mrs. Holmes said. "It's the best."

Zak looked at Mia and felt his face go red.

Mrs. Holmes held out a bottle. Mia took it and poured the contents into the jar. As she did, the brain floated to the surface.

"Drat," Zak said.

"I think we just need to weigh it down," Mia said. She opened her purse, took out some coins, and stuck them inside the gooey imitation sheep brain. After five quarters, four nickels, and four pennies she dropped it back into the oil.

The brain dove, briefly bobbed to the surface, then settled completely submerged in the olive oil, listing to one side.

They cheered.

9

Larry's Little Problem

"You're in trouble," Chloe said, smiling, as Zak entered the house. She sat in one of the chairs that faced the front door wearing a blue and white soccer uniform with blue socks pulled up to the knees.

"You don't know anything," he said.

Larry lay flat on his stomach next to the chair and looked up at Zak with sad eyes, not even wagging his tail.

"Hey, Lar." Larry blinked but did not get up.

Zak's mother stormed into the living room and threw down a dish towel.

"Zak Dale. While we were gone I asked you to do one thing, one simple thing. Do you remember? Of course you don't. You're too busy watching TV or playing with your friends. Having too much fun. When your mother asks you to do something it goes in one ear and out the other."

"What'd I do?"

"What did you do? What did you do?" His mother paced back and forth in front of him. "It's what you didn't do. I asked you to take Larry out while we were at the soccer game. Was it too much to ask? No. We get home and what do we find? Larry sitting next to a puddle of his own urine. Not only that, but there were puddles all over the house. I counted three."

"Oh, yeah. I was going to let him out."

"That's right, Zak. You were going to let him out," she said sarcastically. "We've talked about this before." She looked at Larry, then back at Zak. "Your lack of responsibility, I mean. Well, this has got to stop. Right here and right now."

"But I had a good reason," Zak said, holding out the jar with the imitation brain.

"I told your father to leave the puddles where they are. You're cleaning them up, young man."

"Okay," Zak said. "But I have a good reason."

"You always have a good reason. Well, forgetting isn't a good reason." She paused and walked up to him so she was inches away from his face. "Well? What is it? Tell me the reason."

"I was cleaning the science lab," Zak began.

"We know that. You already told us that."

"And, well, there was a lot to clean."

"Over six hours of cleaning? I don't think so. I can't get you to clean your room for three minutes!"

"I was almost done and then I accidentally dropped this sheep brain all over the floor and it was a big mess so I had to clean that up and then I had to go over to this girl's house so we could make a fake brain so Dr. Fletcher wouldn't know and I can get that summer job I want and that took until just now. See?"

Zak held out the container with the marshmallow brain.

Susan Dale stared at the jar and then at her son.

"What's that?"

"It's a sheep brain. Well, not really. The real one is next to

51

the school dumpster after it fell all over the floor. This is a brain we made out of mini-marshmallows. I'm hoping it'll fool Dr. Fletcher."

"Zak…you…," Mrs. Dale said, flustered. "You should have called."

"Sorry. I forgot. I lost track of time. We just got done a little while ago, and Mrs. Holmes drove me home. I'm sorry."

"Go clean up," Mrs. Dale said. "Wash up, I mean. I'll take care of Larry's little problem."

"I can do it, Mom," Zak said.

"Go wash up. Go."

10

Grandma Morris

"I don't want to hear another word, Chloe," Mr. Dale said. "We're going to see your grandmother. This is non-negotiable."

Sunday morning following church, the Dale family squeezed into their Accord and hopped onto the interstate. Mr. Dale, dressed in a dark gray sport coat and black khaki pants, drove; Mrs. Dale, wearing a teal dress with a white collar, sat in the passenger seat; a pouting Chloe and silent Zak reading a *Sports Illustrated* magazine sat in the back.

"This is stupid," Chloe said.

"How can visiting your grandmother be stupid? She's your family. She loves you," Mrs. Dale said.

"I don't care."

"Well, young lady, you had better start caring. Grandma Morris has done a lot for you—a lot for all of us—and the least you can do is show some appreciation."

"But that place smells," Chloe said. "And there's nothing to do."

"You can tell her about church this morning."

53

"That's boring."

Mr. Dale glanced back quickly. "Did you even listen to the sermon?"

"It was about Jesus, wasn't it?" Chloe said uncertainly.

"You tell us," Mr. Dale said. He checked his blind spot, signaled the turn, and eased into the middle lane of traffic to pass a car on his right.

"I'll give you a hint," Mrs. Dale said as she opened the church bulletin. "The title of the sermon was 'Who Do You Trust?'" She turned her head to face Chloe. "Does that help?"

"I think Pastor Bob said we need to trust Jesus," Chloe said, at first smiling but then frowning. "Why doesn't Zak have to tell what happened? Why is it always me?"

"He said we need to trust God," Zak said, not looking up from his magazine. "He said that whether things are good or bad, we need to trust God. Even if we don't know what's going on."

"Very good, Zak," Mr. Dale said. "I didn't think you were listening."

"That's not fair," Chloe said. "I was going to say that." Then her eyes lit up. "Oh, and he told that story about that one guy and the devil, the one where everybody died."

Mr. Dale put on his right turn signal and steered the car into the right lane of traffic.

"Job," Zak said, looking up. "That whole story doesn't work for me. Job was this good guy who trusted God, and so God turns him over to the devil to mess with."

"Test him," Mr. Dale said.

"Whatever," Zak said. "So Satan kills Job's sheep and camels and sons and daughters. And Job shaves his head and says, 'The Lord gives and the Lord takes away.' What's that about?"

Mr. Dale signaled and brought the car onto the exit ramp. He slowed and stopped at a traffic light, looked for vehicles from the left, and then turned right.

"Job kept his faith even when his world was falling apart," Mrs. Dale said.

"What about the animals? Why did they have to die?" Chloe asked.

"And the rest of the family," Zak said.

"That's not the point," Mrs. Dale said, glancing at her husband. "It's a story about what you believe and the strength of those beliefs. It's about knowing there's something bigger and more important than you are." She quickly added, "But enough about Job. The point I want to make about your grandmother is you need to spend some time with her. Talk to her."

"About Job?" Chloe said.

"Something other than Job," Mrs. Dale said, exasperated.

Bill Dale maneuvered the car into a parking space in front of a large brick building with a red metal roof. The Dales got out of the car and walked to the entrance. A sign identified the building as Green Valley, "an Assisted Living Community." The automatic doors opened as the family approached, and they entered a spacious reception area with oak tables and chairs, large green plants, and windows that filled the area with light.

"See what I mean about the smell?" Chloe whispered.

"Shhh," Mrs. Dale hissed.

Zak liked seeing his grandmother but could never get used to Green Valley. He wondered what it would be like to live in a place like this with old people all around and nothing to do. He remembered her old house in the city where she and Zak's grandfather had lived for years. It had a porch and a big climbing tree in the backyard and the kitchen always smelled like fresh-baked bread and cinnamon. He loved going there. But he always felt knotted up inside at Green Valley.

"Good morning!" the receptionist said. "Should I tell Gloria that you're here?"

"Thank you. We'll just surprise her, if that's okay," Mrs. Dale said.

They walked past a cafeteria area, turned down a long hallway, and stood in front of room 116. A small wreath of dried flowers hung on the door.

Mrs. Dale knocked gently.

"Grandma Morris?" she said, putting her head close to the door. "Grandma Morris? Do you have time for some visitors?"

The door opened slowly and revealed a small, frail woman in a cotton house dress. She had white curly hair, glasses, and an elliptical face. Thin green and blue veins appeared under the pale, wrinkled, almost transparent skin of her neck and arms.

"I didn't expect this," she said, smiling.

Gloria Morris' voice was rich and confident, and her blue eyes twinkled.

"Hi, Grandma Morris," Chloe said.

"Hi, Grandma," Zak said.

"Come in, come in. No reason to stand in the hall."

As Mr. Dale, Chloe, and Zak entered the apartment, Grandma Morris took a quick look down both sides of the hallway. Mrs. Dale paused in the doorway with a puzzled look on her face.

"I was expecting someone else," Grandma Morris said.

"You're making friends?" Mrs. Dale asked.

"Yes, of course," Grandma Morris said. "In fact, I am expecting a visit from Mrs. Miriam Ramsey. She's...new."

Mrs. Dale closed the door and joined the others. The apartment was compact: a living room with pale green carpeting and a view of the parking lot, a small dining table and four chairs, a kitchen with small white appliances, a bedroom with just enough room for a double bed and dresser, and a green and white tiled bathroom.

"It's good to see you, Gloria," Mr. Dale said, giving the elderly woman a gentle hug.

"And nice to know you're meeting more people," Mrs. Dale said.

"I hope you don't mind," Grandma Morris said.

"Mind?" Mrs. Dale said.

"Mrs. Ramsey is…what do you say these days? African American."

"Yes?"

"Your father…he would not have approved," Grandma Morris said in a low voice, shaking her head.

"Approved of what?" Chloe asked.

"Howard didn't like anything different," Grandma Morris said.

"I remember Grandpa used to eat potatoes at dinner every night," Zak said. "And he put ice cubes in his milk."

"I don't remember that," Chloe said. "I don't remember Grandpa Morris at all."

"Oh, he had a terrible prejudice," Grandma Morris said.

"What's prejudice?" Chloe asked.

"It's when people make up their minds about someone because of how they look or act, and not because of who they are," Mr. Dale said.

"It was a different time," Grandma Morris said. "So long ago." They stood in silence for a moment, then Grandma Morris said, "Sit, sit. I have some cookies somewhere. Would anybody like cookies?"

"I would, Grandma Morris," Chloe said.

Zak nodded and sat next to Mr. Dale on a small sofa with a

green floral pattern. Chloe sat on a wooden rocking chair next to the window and stared at a large oil painting of Don Quixote that hung on the wall.

Grandma Morris walked a few steps to the kitchen, swung open one of the cabinet doors, and reached inside. Oreos.

"I believe these are from the last time you were here. But they should still be good."

Mrs. Dale picked up the package and sniffed the contents.

"I'm not sure," Mrs. Dale said.

"They're fine," Grandma Morris said. She arranged the cookies on a plate, selected five paper napkins, and carried them to the living room.

As Zak and Chloe leaned forward, Mrs. Dale said, "Zak, Chloe, wash your hands."

"Why don't adults ever have to wash their hands?" Chloe asked, getting up from the chair.

"We know where our hands have been," Mrs. Dale said.

"I know where mine have been," Chloe said. "Right here on my wrists." She flopped her hands back and forth.

"Go," Mrs. Dale said, rolling her eyes.

"Oh, she's so clever, that little one," Grandma Morris chuckled.

"Not so little any more," Mr. Dale said. "Third grade. It won't be too long before she's in middle school."

"My, my."

"Zak will be a *sophomore* next year."

"A sophomore!" Grandma Morris exclaimed, turning to look at Zak, who was returning from the bathroom and wiping his hands on his jeans.

"You always say that, Grandma," Zak said, taking three cookies from the plate.

"I suppose I do."

Zak sat back in the sofa.

"Sit up straight, Zak," Mrs. Dale said.

Zak sighed and straightened his back a little. Only the toes of his shoes reached the floor.

Grandma Morris looked at Zak and said, "Your grandfather was not a tall man, either. Howard was just under five and a half feet. You remind me so much of him."

Zak tried to hide the pained look that came over his face. He didn't like being reminded of his size.

"Mother," Mrs. Dale said. "How are things going here? Do they look in on you? Is the food good?"

"It's fine, fine. I'm still making adjustments—I get turned around, sometimes—but I'm getting along. People are so nice."

Zak looked at the small apartment. It seemed sterile and incomplete. He tried to figure out what was missing. It felt temporary, he decided. It didn't feel like a home.

In the silence, Chloe said, "Larry peed all over the house because Zak forgot about him yesterday."

"Chloe!" Mrs. Dale snapped.

"I'm just making conversation."

"Make it about something else," Mr. Dale said.

A knock on the door brought Gloria Morris to her feet. Chloe followed close behind.

"Can I open the door, Grandma?"

"Of course you may."

Chloe turned the handle and pulled the door back to reveal a squat, elderly, dark-skinned woman wearing a black dress and a string of shiny white pearls around her neck. She held an envelope in her left hand and a simple wooden cane in her right.

"I'm so sorry. I didn't realize you had company, Gloria," the woman said in a slow, deliberate, husky voice. "I will come again another time."

"Miriam, please come in. I'd like to introduce you to my family," Grandma Morris said.

"You must be Grandma's new friend," Chloe said, holding out her hand. "She's never had a friend like you before, on account of Grandpa being prejudice and all."

"Your grandmother is a special woman," Mrs. Ramsey said, taking the girl's hand in her own. "I enjoy her company very much." She leaned down to look at Chloe's face. "What is your name, young lady?"

"My name is Chloe Elizabeth Dale and I am pleased to meet you."

"My name is Miriam Harriet Truth Ramsey. The pleasure is mine."

"You have four names?"

"Yes I do. It was a lot of letters to grow into."

"I wish I had another name like you."

Mrs. Ramsey straightened up and repositioned her cane.

"Such a delightful child, Gloria."

Grandma Morris escorted Miriam Ramsey into the room.

"This is my daughter, Susan Dale. My son-in-law, Bill Dale. And my grandson, Zak."

They nodded and shook hands.

"It's so nice to see that Mother is meeting new people," Mrs. Dale said.

"Gloria has made me feel so welcome here."

"Miriam has given me a new sense of adventure," Grandma Morris said enthusiastically. "We have special plans."

"It arrived," Miriam Ramsey said to Gloria Morris. She held a thick envelope close to her left ear and shook it like a rattle. "It came yesterday."

"I'm so excited," Grandma Morris said. Her eyes lit up, then she turned to Mrs. Dale. "We're planning a little driving trip."

"A trip?" Mr. Dale said.

"I'm sure you don't mean that, Mother," Mrs. Dale said. "You're 82 years old."

"I have a red convertible," Miriam Ramsey said. "If you look out the window, you can see it in the parking lot."

"Awesome," Zak said.

11

Feng Shui

"Dr. Fletcher?"

"Mr. Dale? I didn't expect to see you here so early?"

Zak stood in front of the door to Dr. Fletcher's science room. He'd been waiting in that spot in the nearly-empty school since 6:00. His entire body was stiff and sore after sitting on the floor for nearly an hour.

"Things went well this weekend, I expect?" Dr. Fletcher said.

"I think so? I think you'll like it?"

"Shall we take a look, then?"

Zak nodded.

Dr. Fletcher leaned forward. His big fish eyes were inches away from Zak's face.

"Mr. Dale, it would speed things along enormously if you moved aside so I am able to unlock the door, don't you think?"

"Oh. Sorry," Zak said. He took a few steps to his right and breathed deeply.

Dr. Fletcher put the key in the lock and opened the door. Zak felt a rush of adrenalin. He closed his eyes, opened them, then turned to look into the room as the teacher flipped on the light switch.

"Quite a difference, quite a difference, wouldn't you say?" Dr. Fletcher said, quickly examining the clean, organized room.

"I cleaned the whiteboard, Dr. Fletcher."

"I can see that."

"I washed the windows, Dr. Fletcher."

"Yes?"

"And all the test tubes, flasks, beakers, and Petri dishes."

"Very good, very good."

"Um…," Zak began, and then, in a loud voice, said, "I did have a question about the Bunsen burners." He paused. Then, even louder, Zak repeated, "The Bunsen burners."

"I heard you, Mr. Dale. The Bunsen burners? What is your question?"

"Over here," Zak said, tugging at his teacher's suit coat and directing him toward the far corner of the room where several Bunsen burners were lined up on a table.

At that moment, Mia Holmes—dressed in black jeans, black tennis shoes, and a black turtleneck—slipped into the room carrying the glass jar with the imitation brain. Zak looked past Dr. Fletcher and saw Mia flash him a quick smile.

"I wasn't quite sure where to put the Bunsen burners, Dr. Fletcher." Zak spoke slowly and loudly as if his teacher were hard of hearing. "You can see that I put them over here, but"—Zak motioned toward the table—"they could go just about anywhere, I think. I mean…"

"It really doesn't matter, Mr. Dale," Dr. Fletcher interrupted.

"It's a question of balance, don't you think?" Zak looked hard into Dr. Fletcher's fish eyes.

"Balance?"

Mia Holmes quietly worked her way to the back of the classroom. She looked up at the other jars and the waxy face of Felix the armadillo, who seemed to watch her every move. She set down the brain-filled container, lifted herself onto the countertop, and placed the jar with the imitation sheep brain between the cow eyeballs and the blank-eyed, bean-shaped fetal pig. She looked critically at the arrangement, nodded, and then lowered herself noiselessly to the floor.

"Have you ever heard of feng shui?" Zak asked. "It's a way of looking at where things are placed. I saw something about it on TV once."

"I do not know what you are talking about, Mr. Dale."

"It's just…I didn't know where to put the Bunsen burners, Dr. Fletcher. Do you see my point? I want the energy to be right. We don't want bad energy."

Zak could feel the sweat drip from his armpits and his hands started to shake.

"Mr. Dale, I believe the energy in this classroom is under control."

Mia crouched low and moved between the desks like a sleek black cat.

"What about the Bunsen burners? I mean, who is this Bunsen anyway?"

"Calm down, Mr. Dale. The Bunsen burner is named after Robert Bunsen, a German chemist. I believe he made an appearance on one of our examinations?"

Mia Holmes gave a small wave as she slipped out the door.

"That's fascinating, Dr. Fletcher," Zak said, relief in his voice. Zak's arms dropped listlessly to his sides and his entire body began to tremble nervously. "I think I need to get to my locker."

Zak inched toward the door.

"A moment, Mr. Dale?"

"Yes?"

Dr. Fletcher scanned the room and then sniffed.

"Do you smell something, Mr. Dale?"

"I'm sure I don't, Dr. Fletcher."

"I have a very sensitive nose, did you know that?"

"I…I didn't. That's interesting. Um, congratulations."

Zak steeled himself for questions and accusations as the teacher sniffed the air again.

"Very pleasant. Citrus. Almost like perfume. Nice touch."

Zak sighed.

"You did a remarkable job. Well done, Mr. Dale?"

"Um, thanks. Thank you, Dr. Fletcher."

As he left the room, Zak looked up at Felix and thought he saw the stuffed armadillo wink.

12

Causes of War

Mia and Zak stood outside their first hour American History classroom, whispering.

"I couldn't think what I was going to say next," Zak said.

"Feng shui?" Mia said, amused.

Zak looked for crooked teeth but still didn't see any.

"It was all I could think of," he said. She smiled again and Zak sniffed the air. He smelled Citronesia perfume. "By the way, what's with the Goth look?" Zak said, gesturing to Mia's black outfit.

"It's not Goth. It's ninja. Or," she added, "retro jewel thief."

"Oh. Yeah. Right." Zak nodded. "That's what I meant to say."

They both looked at the clock, nodded to each other, then went to their desks and watched as Mr. Brown wrote "Causes of the American Revolution" on the whiteboard. At the sound of the bell the rest of the students went to their desks and faced the front as Mr. Brown turned to study his class.

"There is much history to cover today," Darius Brown said loudly, trying to be heard over the lingering buzz of conversations.

"As you may have guessed, in this subject, every day we get further and further behind."

Zak thought about that. Every day, every second that passed became history. It felt strange to be part of that, even a small part. All those seconds added up to something that he shared with every person who had ever lived. Abraham Lincoln and Julius Caesar and Babe Ruth were all part of the same history. They were real people a lot like him.

"Causes of the American Revolution...Miss Daniels," Mr. Brown said.

"Yes?" Candice Daniels responded.

"Please name one of the causes if you can."

"It's...that test was a long time ago," she said.

"So was the American Revolution," he said.

The class laughed.

"Mr. Koll," Darius Brown said, looking at the seating chart and then back up at the mammoth football player who sat in front of Zak.

"Huh?"

"You were absent on Friday."

"Yeah," Jeremiah Koll said. "It's my knee. I had to get it x-rayed."

"Can you help us with the causes of the American Revolution?"

"Where's that other teacher? That Jackson lady?" Jeremiah asked.

"She is no longer teaching this class." Darius Brown looked around the classroom and tried to make eye contact with several students, then he turned back to Jeremiah. "Let me put this another way," he said. "What would cause you, Mr. Koll, to revolt against the King of England?"

"I wouldn't do that," Jeremiah said. He sat up a little in his chair.

"Why not?"

"I got nothing against the guy," he said.

"Suppose you did?" Darius Brown asked.

Maggie Cho's arm shot up.

"Yes," Mr. Brown said, looking down at the seating chart and back up at Maggie Cho, "Miss Cho?"

"Wasn't it 'taxation without representation'?" she asked. "Isn't that what started it?"

"Very good," Mr. Brown said. "Taxation. Yes. But what does that mean?" He scanned the class. "Mr. Preston?"

Fuzz looked up. "Huh?" he said. The class laughed.

"Why would taxation be a cause of the American Revolution?"

"It's all about money, isn't it?" Fuzz Preston said. "I mean, I got mine and you can't have it."

"But without taxes you don't have police, fire departments, libraries, schools, and sewers. Taxes do a lot of good." He looked at the seating chart. "Is that right, Miss Holmes?"

"I suppose," Mia said quietly. "Taxes can do good things."

"So why not pay?"

"Not all taxes are good," Mia said.

"For example?"

"Taxes that people can't afford," Mia said. "Or that support things people don't need or want. Those would be bad."

"Another example, Miss Ramerez."

"A tax that helps the King," Katie Ramerez said.

"Elvis?" Fuzz Preston said.

"King George the Third," Darius Brown said, glaring at Fuzz. Mr. Brown craned his neck to locate Zak behind the hulking figure of Jeremiah Koll. "Mr. Dale?"

Zak was always startled to hear his name. Most teachers

ignored him, and he liked it that way.

"I suppose a tax that helps England and not America," Zak said. "That would be an example."

"And the army," Fuzz Preston said. "Paying for the army."

"Isn't the army one of the benefits of your taxes, like the police and fire department? Doesn't it protect you from your enemies?"

"Unless you're the enemy," Zak said quietly.

"What did you say? Speak up, Mr. Dale."

"I said, unless you're the enemy," Zak said. "Americans, I mean. Not you."

"Interesting observation, Mr. Dale." There was silence, and then Darius Brown continued. "You pay taxes to help yourself and your family and your friends. And to protect you from your enemies."

"That's the representation part, though, isn't it?" said Arlo Mould, a boy with unruly black hair and a large brown mole on his cheek that earned him the nickname Moleman.

"It is, Mr. ...," Darius Brown looked to the seating chart, but Arlo Mould said, "Mould" first. "Yes. Mr. Mould. Thank you." Darius Brown loosened his necktie. "Tell me about 'the representation part.'"

"It's just that if it's your money, you should have a say in where it goes."

"Otherwise?"

"We're not free. We're like slaves," Candice Daniels said. "So it is about slavery after all."

"Some did call it slavery," Darius Brown said. He picked up a worn, stained American history textbook, turned a few pages, and ran his finger down one of the columns. "Thomas Paine wrote, 'Britain, with an army to enforce her tyranny, has declared that she has a right (not only to TAX) but "to BIND us in ALL CASES

WHATSOEVER" and if being bound in that manner is not slavery, then is there not such a thing as slavery upon the earth.' Paine was trying to make a point, and to get the colonists angry by suggesting they were slaves to Great Britain. He is not talking about African slaves."

"It's about freedom," Jason Wiley said.

"Freedom," Darius Brown repeated. "How do you feel when somebody tells you what to do? When it's not fair? Mr. Koll?"

"Me again? Ms. Jackson never said nothing to me the whole time. She left me alone."

"I'm asking you, Mr. Koll, because I value your opinion."

"Okay, okay," Jeremiah said. He wiped his forehead and face with a large hand. "When somebody tells me what to do and it's not fair...I get mad. I want to hit somebody."

"Mr. Koll wants to hit somebody," Darius Brown said. "Anybody else?"

"I let Jer hit whatever he wants to hit," Bruce Fetzlof, a running back on the junior varsity football team, said, grinning. "Just get behind him. That's what I'd do."

"We have two patriots willing to fight for independence, then." Darius Brown studied the seating chart. "We haven't heard from a few others here. What would you do, Miss Taylor?"

Trudy Taylor was a quiet, mousy girl with bright red hair. A swarm of copper-colored freckles covered her chalk-white skin. Her face turned red when her name was mentioned.

"I...don't...think...I'd...do...anything," she said slowly.

"Nothing?"

Trudy Taylor shook her head.

"I'd complain to my friends," Betty Ng said. "Send 'em texts and talk to them."

"That's what Thomas Paine did. The gentleman I just quoted.

He wrote, 'These are the times that try men's souls.' Is that what you'd say?"

"No. I'd say how unfair it is and that we need to do something about it," Betty Ng said. "Oh, and to spread the word."

"Who is this Paine guy?" Martee Freeman asked.

"Pain in the neck," Fuzz Preston said.

"That he was, Mr. Preston. To the British he was a pain in the neck. Today Miss Ng would be writing, complaining, and stirring up trouble. Back then it was Thomas Paine and others." Darius Brown looked at his watch and then at the clock. "In 1776, Thomas Paine printed a pamphlet called 'Common Sense,' which was an attack on King George the Third. Keep in mind that there were no televisions, no radios, no cell phones, no internet. Just speeches and writing." Darius Brown picked up his textbook. "This piece of paper…"—he loudly tore five pages from his already-distressed American history textbook—"got people angry and thinking and acting and believing."

"You just tore your book," Beth Sanders said.

"Yes."

"Why did you do that?" she asked, shocked.

Mr. Brown laughed. "I want you to remember the importance of the printed word in history. Without paper and ink, it is likely that this revolution would never have happened."

"But your book…," she said.

"My book will be fine. The words are still there," Darius Brown said, holding up the pages. "Now, I just have a couple of minutes left, so here are some facts. In 1770 there were about 1.7 million men, women, and children in America. And in England? Fewer than six million. Our population was growing fast—doubling about every 25 years."

"I bet that was scary for the King," Beth Sanders said.

"America is more than 3,000 miles from England," Darius Brown said, again looking at his watch. "And many times the size of England."

"Seems like a lost cause," Mia Holmes said. "Too big and too far. Especially back then."

"Here's the real problem," Darius Brown said. "British Parliament and King George thought of America not as a nation but as a territory whose sole purpose was to enhance the wealth of England. They had debts to pay from the French and Indian War here in North America—protecting the colonies from the French—so why not have the colonies pay for that protection?"

"That's not fair," Randy Caton said. "No wonder there was a revolution."

"Parliament—the British government—changed the rules. Up until then they left the colonies pretty much on their own to govern themselves. But now they wanted to step in and collect taxes. In Britain, since 1215 and Magna Carta, citizens had been governed by the principle of 'no taxation without representation.' It was a right. But apparently not a right afforded the colonists."

"I don't get it," Maggie Cho said.

"Think of England as the mother country and America as one of her children. Everything that we produce and do is for her benefit. That's what the English rulers thought," Darius Brown said. "So what happens? Like a good parent, Great Britain wants to control American trade—so they can make more money—which is why we get things like the Navigation Acts. They don't want us to go west beyond Virginia—too hard and expensive to control—that's the Proclamation of 1763. The Sugar Act taxed sugar and coffee and rum. The Stamp Act was a tax on legal documents, newspapers, calendars, ads, and even playing cards. And the Townshend Act taxed paint, paper, glass, and tea."

"Like I said, it's all about the money," Fuzz Preston said.

"You're right, Mr. Preston. You can talk about the ideals of freedom and liberty, but money is often at the heart of it all."

Darius Brown walked down the third aisle, past Jeremiah Koll, and looked at Zak sitting in his chair. "Mr. Dale," he said, "please summarize everything that's been said here today. You have two minutes."

Zak peeked out from behind the large football player to look at the back of his teacher who was now walking toward the front of the classroom. Zak saw everyone looking at him. Fuzz Preston pointed to his wristwatch and mouthed the words, "Two minutes."

"I think," Zak said nervously. He didn't know what to say.

"Go ahead, Mr. Dale," Darius Brown said softly.

His mind was blank, but he started talking.

"Um, I think that America—Americans, I mean—were tired of being treated like kids and told what to do and to pay taxes that didn't seem fair. Parliament kind of went too far." He noticed that Mia Holmes was looking at him with an intense expression, as though she was actually interested in what he was saying. "The Americans felt like they were grown up. They wanted to be treated with respect. And Parliament wanted to make us pay for their war, and didn't give us any choice." He stopped for a moment and then, surprised at his own thought, added, "I guess that's when the people here really started to think of themselves as Americans."

The bell rang. Almost as one, the class grabbed their bags and darted into the hallway. Zak, alone in an island of abandoned chairs, sat for a several seconds after the ringing had stopped.

"Thank you, Mr. Dale," Darius Brown said. "Succinct and incisive. You continue to impress."

Zak nodded, picked up his books, and headed to his English class.

13

Humming the Kitchen Electric

"Bill, the electricity is out again!" Mrs. Dale shouted from the kitchen. "That's the second time this month."

As Mrs. Dale unplugged the toaster and turned off the oven, Mr. Dale came into the kitchen from the living room. His face showed a mixture of irritation and hopelessness. He flipped the light switch off and on several times and stared at the light fixture on the ceiling. Nothing.

"Is the power out again?" Zak said, walking into the kitchen. "The computer cut out on me." He went to the refrigerator to get some food, but his mother stepped in front of him.

"Sorry," she said.

"But I'm hungry," Zak whined.

"We can't risk everything spoiling," Mrs. Dale said.

"I'm going to check the circuit breaker panel," Mr. Dale said.

Mr. Dale took a flashlight from the top of the refrigerator, opened the door to the basement, and went downstairs while Mrs. Dale and Zak waited.

"Hey, people!" Chloe shouted, storming into the kitchen with a pink towel around her shoulders and a Hello Kitty hair dryer in her hand. "Is there a problem with the 'lectricity? I got some wet hair here." Her light brown hair hung in wet strings and she dripped onto the floor.

"Your father is checking downstairs," Mrs. Dale said to Chloe.

A minute later Mr. Dale reappeared, breathing hard after climbing the stairs.

"I don't know what the problem is," he said between breaths. "We'll have to call Mark."

"Now my hair is never gonna get dry," Chloe exclaimed, setting the hair dryer on the counter and walking back toward her room.

"This is getting old, Bill," Mrs. Dale said.

"I know," Mr. Dale said. He looked around the kitchen from appliance to appliance, then at the robin's egg blue paint on the walls, and finally outside at the yellow glow of the sun through the maple trees in the backyard. "We need another electrician."

"One that actually fixes things," Zak said.

"This is hard," Mr. Dale said, shaking his head. "It's like… betraying a friend."

"He's our neighbor, not our friend," Mrs. Dale said.

"I just wish he didn't live across the street," Mr. Dale said. "Every time this happens we give Mark a call and he comes over late at night and takes two hours to drink beer, get the power back on, and watch TV. It's like some kind of social event."

"And that humming. I can't stand that," Mrs. Dale said. "Whenever he's 'working' on something he's always humming."

"And you can see his underwear," Zak said. "White boxers with red hearts."

"I talked to Patty Jones and she gave me the name of an electrician she uses," Mrs. Dale said, picking up a note from the

75

kitchen counter and handing it to her husband.

Mr. Dale walked through the dining room to the living room, the walls of which were covered with photos of family members. Mrs. Dale and Zak followed. Bill Dale looked at the phone number on the note and then at the house across the street. A white van was parked in the driveway with "Mark Snyder, Electric" in big orange and black letters on the side.

"He's probably watching us right now," Mrs. Dale said.

"Maybe we can do it without him knowing," Mr. Dale said.

"How do you do that? He and Judy can look out their window and see a truck in the driveway. When it gets dark it'll be pretty obvious. He'll be sitting by the phone waiting for us to call."

"Sounds like a horror movie," Zak said.

14

Trivia

"Mr. Brown?" Nicole Anderson's hand shot up. "Mr. Brown, um, I have a question."

Darius Brown finished writing the word "Independence" on the whiteboard and turned to face his first period American History class. Most students continued to talk in low voices. Zak sat in his usual chair eclipsed by Jeremiah Koll. He tried to catch Mia Holmes' eye, but all he could see was the back of her head.

"Yes, Miss Anderson," Mr. Brown said.

"I was just wondering when we'll get our tests back."

"Your tests?"

"The last one we did for Ms. Jackson. On the Civil War and Reconstruction."

"Yes," Mr. Brown said slowly, dragging out each letter as if it were its own word. "I did review those tests, of course."

"That test sucked," Jason Wiley said.

"I don't even remember it," Katie Ramerez said.

"Ms. Jackson said it counted for one-third of our grade," Nicole Anderson said.

"Well, Miss Anderson, there is no need to concern yourself any more." Darius Brown looked down at his shoes and then back up. "That test has been…discarded."

"You threw it out?" Betty Ng said in disbelief.

The classroom became unusually quiet. Heads that rested against desks suddenly bobbed up, shook, and stared ahead, as if witness to some horrible automobile accident.

"Actually, your tests were not thrown away. They were recycled. I can only hope they will be reborn as better examinations."

"But you can't do that," Nicole Anderson said. "I…I studied really hard for that test."

"I did not think that particular test addressed the most important issues of the American Civil War. Nor did the scores accurately reflect the quality of work I have observed since becoming your teacher," Mr. Brown said. "Surprisingly, Mr. Koll, Mr. Dale, Miss Ramerez, Mr. Preston, and others did not perform as well as would be expected. These students were no less smart a month ago, so I must assume there was a problem with the test."

Fuzz Preston said, "Cool." Zak sighed in relief. Katie Ramerez slid down in her chair and rubbed her eyebrows. Jeremiah Koll nodded vigorously and punched the air with his fist.

"But…," began Nicole Anderson.

"In my opinion, this test did not cover the critical issues of the Civil War," Darius Brown said.

"That's not fair," Martee Freeman said.

Darius Brown sighed and looked around the classroom.

"Tell me," Darius Brown said. "What was the name of Abraham Lincoln's wife. Mr. Caton?"

Randy Caton shook his head.

"Anybody?

"Mary," Beth Sanders said. "Mary Todd."

"Correct," Darius Brown said. "Now tell me, why is that bit of information important? Miss Taylor?"

"Me?"

"Yes. What does Mary Todd Lincoln have to do with the most divisive war in the history of this nation? Why was that question on your test?"

"Um. She was Abraham Lincoln's wife," Trudy Taylor said quietly.

"Did she fight any battles? Draft any legislation? Counsel the president? Was she a diplomat or a spy? Did she save hundreds of lives?"

"I...I don't know," Trudy Taylor said nervously. "I don't think so."

"Let me tell you something," Darius Brown began quietly. "Many women have figured prominently in the history of this country. Abigail Adams, Margaret Corbin, Polly Cooper, Clara Barton, Susan B. Anthony, Sojourner Truth, Mary Elizabeth Bowser, Maria Isabella Boyd, and others. Tens of thousands of others. Not Mary Todd Lincoln. Memorizing the name Mary Todd Lincoln for a test on the American Civil War marginalizes the contributions of every woman who has changed the course of history in this country." Darius Brown stepped forward, straightened his necktie, and cleared his throat. "Mary Todd Lincoln is trivia."

The class was silent. Ten seconds went by.

"Ms. Jackson must have had a reason," Candice Daniels said.

"I have nothing against Ms. Jackson. I don't know her. But I do know that this American History class is about important people, events, and ideas. It is not about common men and women or obscure dates you will forget the instant you walk out of this room. We do not have time to waste on inconsequential figures like Mary Todd Lincoln."

"So what do you really think?" Fuzz Preston said, chuckling.

"Another question from your test," Darius Brown said. "Tell me...what famous Civil War figure is on the $50 bill?"

"I've never seen one of them," Dez Mitchell said, smiling. He was normally face down asleep at his desk, but now he was awake and engaged.

"Ulysses S. Grant," Moleman said.

"Important...or trivia?"

"Grant was important," Tom Gleason said.

"But not that he's on the $50 bill," Zak said.

"Correct, Mr. Dale," Mr. Brown said. "And—another question from the test—how many soldiers were killed or injured at the battle of Gettysburg? Fifty, 500, 5,000, or 50,000?"

"I think it was like 50,000, wasn't it?" Tom Gleason said.

"That's right, Mr. Gleason. About 51,000 is a commonly accepted number," Mr. Brown said. "Important...or trivia?"

"Trivia!"

"Not so fast," Mr. Brown said quickly. "Gettysburg was the deadliest battle of the Civil War. Casualties totaled about 28,000 soldiers from the South and about 23,000 soldiers from the North."

"That many?" Nick Draves said.

"Yes, Mr. ..."

"Draves. Nick Draves."

"About 51,000 soldiers in all, Mr. Draves. And more than 3,000 horses died as well."

"Three thousand horses died?" Martee Freeman said, shocked.

"We didn't learn that," Maggie Cho said.

"More trivia," Mia Holmes said. "The horses, I mean."

"Exactly, Miss Holmes," Darius Brown said. "But the battle itself was a turning point in the war. Did you learn about that?"

"I think so," Beth Sanders said. "I mean, it was in some of the DVDs we watched."

"In July, in 1863, General Robert E. Lee of the Confederate Army wanted to disrupt the Union Army commanded by General George Meade."

"How do you remember all this stuff?" Jeremiah Koll asked, shaking his head.

"Start with the basics, Mr. Koll—what's really important—and keep filling in the blanks. The thing to remember is that it is a story. History is a story."

"A boring story," Randy Caton said.

"It doesn't have to be boring, Mr. Caton," Darius Brown said. "The Civil War was a battle of America against itself. Remember the question we were asking about the American Revolution: who are we and who do we want to be? We're still trying to figure that out. In the Civil War, both sides had a different answer. Both sides thought what they believed was worth fighting and dying for. The poet Walt Whitman wrote, 'Do I contradict myself? Very well, then I contradict myself, I am large, I contain multitudes.'" Mr. Brown stopped and looked around the classroom. "'I contain multitudes.' That is America."

"Do we have to remember any of this?" Moleman asked.

"In Gettysburg, Pennsylvania, the North kept the South from advancing. Lee's army was forced to go back to Virginia. That's important. And it's also important that 51,000 people were killed or injured."

"But what was so important that all those people had to die?" Betty Ng asked.

"Miss Ng, that is precisely the question you need to ask about history, all history: why? Why, why, why?" Darius Brown said. "Can anybody answer Miss Ng's question? Miss Daniels?"

"Slavery?" Candice Daniels asked sheepishly.

"That's part of it," Darius Brown said. "Here's the question from your test: which was not a major cause of the Civil War? Economic disparity, states rights, slavery, or Canada." Mr. Brown looked around the classroom. "Mr. Fetzlof."

Bruce Fetzlof shook his head. "Dunno."

"Take a guess."

"I didn't understand all that Civil War stuff," Bruce Fetzlof said. "Betty the Brain knows. Ask her."

"You have a one out of four chance, Mr. Fetzlof," Darius Brown said.

Bruce Fetzlof shook his head.

"Ms. Daniels identified slavery as one of the causes, so it's really a one in three chance."

"That test was a long time ago," Bruce Fetzlof said. He looked from side to side. His eyes met Jeremiah Koll's.

"Go for it, man," Jeremiah said.

"Okay, okay," he said. "What are my choices again?"

"The question is: which was *not* a major cause of the American Civil War? Not a cause, Mr. Fetzlof," Darius Brown said. "Economic differences between the North and the South." He held up one finger. "Whether the states should have more control than the federal government." He held up two fingers. "The question of slavery." He held up three fingers. "Or Canada." He held up four fingers.

Nicole Anderson laughed. Darius Brown turned his head quickly to glare at her, then turned back to Bruce Fetzlof.

"I…I think Canada," Bruce Fetzlof said.

"That is correct. Canada was not a major cause of the American Civil War," Darius Brown said. "Thank you, Mr. Fetzlof. You aced the test."

"For real?"

"In the mid-1800s there were profound differences between the North and the South. In order to understand the American Civil War, you must understand those differences. You also need to know about States Rights and the abolitionists. And you should know the major players, the Abraham Lincolns and Jefferson Davises, the Robert E. Lees and Ulysses S. Grants. You should know the key battles and why they were important: Bull Run, Sharpsburg, Shiloh, Chancellorville, Gettysburg. Know the economic and cultural differences. And know what's in the hearts and souls of the men and women at the time. Once you understand all that, you have the basis for understanding the American Civil War. One multiple choice question is unacceptable."

Darius Brown glanced at the clock and leaned back against his desk.

"Miss Anderson, please summarize."

"What? Summarize what?"

"Today's discussion."

All heads turned toward Nicole Anderson.

"Well," she began, "we're not getting our tests back, even though some of us studied really, really hard." Nicole Anderson looked at Darius Brown. He smiled. "And about the Civil War, there were a lot of reasons for the war like slavery, the differences between the North and the South, and that thing about the states. But not Canada. Oh…3,000 horses died in the Gettysburg battle. And Mary Todd Lincoln is overrated."

"Nicely done, Miss Anderson," Darius Brown said. "Class, in your study of history I caution all of you, do not get bogged down in trivia."

The bell rang and the class rose as one.

"Tomorrow, back to the American Revolution."

15

Between Lives

At 9:00 in the evening, Zak lay on his bed trying to work his way through *Of Mice and Men* for his English class. Piles of worn clothes were scattered everywhere around him on the floor. His desk was stacked with books and graphic novels and CDs and a few vinyl records from Cream and the Kinks. Posters of Batman, Dr. Who, and Jack White stuck to the walls at odd angles. Food wrappers, Coke cans, and empty potato chip bags filled random spaces. He lay on his bed with the window open. A cool breeze ruffled the pages of a few stray magazines and newspapers. Music played on his computer and the screensaver sent up fireworks every few seconds.

His phone rang. He looked at the screen: Mia Holmes. Zak tossed his book down, shook his head, combed his hair with his fingers, and then answered.

"Hello?"

"Z?"

The voice was hard to hear.

"Mia? Is that you?"

"Uh-huh."

"Is something wrong?"

"No," she said quietly. "No. It's just…no, not really."

"You don't sound like yourself."

"It's just that everything is different. Since we moved. With the new school, new friends, new house…and my dad away so much. And Mom…she'll be back by 11:00, she said."

"Yeah. That has to be weird."

"Mom left a while ago and I turned on all the lights in the house. And the TVs. It helped…a little. I have this feeling of being, I don't know…left…discarded."

"Um…I can come over, if you want," Zak said.

"Just now I was sitting at the piano trying to make noise. I can't even play," she said. "And then suddenly I'm lost. I don't know where I go. Where I fit. That's when I called."

"Look, I'll be over. It'll only take a few minutes."

Zak hurried down the hallway to the living room where his parents were watching television.

"I need to go over to Mia Holmes' house," he said quickly.

"A girl?" Mr. Dale asked, surprised.

"It's 9:00," Mrs. Dale said.

"She's there on her own. Sounds scared."

"It's a weeknight, Zak," Mr. Dale said. "You can't stay too late."

"Her Mom's supposed to be back by 11:00."

"Do you want us to drive you over?" Mrs. Dale asked.

"I'll be okay," Zak said. "I'll take my bike."

"Watch out," Mr. Dale said. "Cars can't see you."

Zak went past the kitchen and opened the door to the garage.

"And wear your helmet, Zak," Mrs. Dale shouted after him.

"Right," Zak said.

Zak located his bike in the dark garage and wheeled it out the side door. He hopped on, unhelmeted, and rode the mile and a half to Mia's home.

The house was just as Mia had said. Every light had been turned on inside and out so it glowed like a giant lantern. Zak set his bike in the grass and went up the steps to the front door. As he rang the doorbell he could hear the televisions. He looked through the narrow pane of glass to the right of the door and saw Mia sitting on the piano bench. He knocked hard on the glass and watched as she turned around. Her face lit up when she saw him. That was a new experience for Zak. He was used to people ignoring or, at most, barely recognizing him. He'd never had the feeling that someone actually wanted to see him.

The door opened and Mia stood barefoot, wearing a T-shirt and jeans and an open bathrobe and eyeglasses. Her hair was pulled back into a short ponytail.

"Hi," Mia said as she looked at him through the glass of the storm door.

"Hi."

"Do you want to come in?"

"Sure."

Zak pulled open the door and went into the house. He noticed the spotless entry, the crystal chandelier above his head, the hardwood floors, a closet, and a small oil painting of a boat on a lake. The shiny black baby grand piano stood in a room just off the entry with pages of music scattered around it. The sound from the televisions was deafening.

"You got rid of all the boxes," Zak shouted, looking around.

"Boxes? Oh, from the move. Yeah. My mom always has everything organized," Mia shouted back.

Zak nodded. "It looks nice."

Mia sighed.

"I'm sorry about the call," she said. Zak strained to hear her voice. "I never felt the move until now." She lowered her head, then tilted it up to look Zak in the eyes. "It's like I'm in between lives or something."

"It has to be strange to move your whole life like that," Zak said.

"Do you want something to drink?"

"Yeah. That sounds good."

Mia walked through the entry with Zak behind her. She turned off the television in the kitchen, opened the refrigerator, and handed Zak a Pepsi.

"I hope you don't think I'm crazy."

"At first I thought you were on drugs."

"Seriously?"

"That's what it sounded like. All quiet and hazy and new age, and all the noise in the background."

She laughed.

"Let's go into the living room. I have to turn off the TV in there, too."

Zak followed Mia into the living room. She grabbed a remote control and pointed it at the television, which went blank. The house was suddenly eerily quiet.

"I see what you mean about the silence," Zak said.

"Yeah," she said, plopping herself down onto a dark brown leather chair and pulling one leg up underneath her. "I was just sitting here and it was getting to me. I'm not used to this."

"Do you want to go back to your old house?" Zak sat on the matching couch on the side closest to Mia. He looked around for a place to put his drink and settled on a *Time* magazine.

"I thought so at first," she said. "I cried a lot. And threw some things. It wasn't pretty."

"And now?"

"I don't know," she said, sighing. "There's friends I left behind. And the house I grew up in. And I was busy with so many things—basketball, volleyball, student government, speech, debate."

"You were in all that?" Zak was amazed.

Mia nodded.

"Do you want to see a picture of my old house?" she asked, jumping up from the chair and disappearing through a hallway.

Zak stood up, not sure what to do. He looked around at the walls, which were decorated with paintings and photographs. Zak wandered toward the big stone fireplace and looked at a family portrait on the mantel. He recognized Mia's mother, who was a good deal younger when the picture was taken. She stood next to a man with dark hair and glasses and a big smile. He held a small, blonde-headed girl with a tuft of hair that stood straight up like the hair on a Dr. Seuss character. It was Mia. She was probably two or three years old.

"Here it is," Mia said, coming back into the living room holding a photo that appeared to have been handled many times.

Zak pointed a finger at the old family photograph.

"I was looking at the picture of your family," Zak said.

"My mom just loves that. But do you see my nose—it's huge! And my hair! I think I threw up right after that was taken."

"I like it," Zak said.

Mia moved next to Zak and showed him the photograph in her hand.

"This is where we used to live," she said, pointing to a large white stucco house.

"In Wisconsin?"

Mia nodded.

"There's a big tree in back and a swing set and we even had a vegetable garden and apple trees."

Zak held the photograph in his hands. The house was older, and he could see the side of another house to one side. There were yellow and red flowers and a bumpy green lawn and a big pine tree on the other side. It wasn't a suburban development like Golden Meadows. It looked more comfortable, more permanent.

"It looks a lot different than this house," Zak said.

Mia took the photograph from Zak and gripped it tightly on either side with both hands.

"That's part of who I am right there."

"Why did you move?"

"My dad took a job with a company here in the Cities. I don't really know what he does. Senior Marketing Manager is what his business card says. All I know is that he's away a lot more." She walked slowly back to the leather chair and sat down on the edge of one of the arms, still looking at the photograph.

"I don't know what to say," Zak said.

"Thanks for being here," she said. Then she reached out and squeezed his hand.

"Sure," he said, embarrassed.

She looked up, laughed, and then frisbeed the photo across the room.

"I shouldn't let the past drag me down like that."

"I never noticed before. You're left handed," Zak said.

"My dad always wanted a left-handed pitcher," Mia said. "He used to call me 'Southpaw.' And then just 'South.'"

"South," Zak said, musing. "I like that. My real name is too long. Zacchaeus."

"That's your name? Zacchaeus?" Mia asked, grinning.

"Yeah," he said. "My parents wanted something that began with 'Z.' I don't know why." Zak shook his head. "And there aren't a lot of options."

"I like 'Z.' It's cool."

There was a long pause.

"I should probably go home," Zak said.

"We could watch a movie," Mia said.

"Sure," Zak said, eagerly. "But I have to leave when your mom gets home. Like my parents said, it's a school night and all."

"You didn't have to come over, Z," Mia said.

"Yes, I did."

16

Minefield

Zak saw him first.

As Zak passed the kitchen window, he noticed something move in the backyard. He took a few steps toward the glass and watched a short, balding man with a large canvas bag dart through the lilac bushes. The man looked from side to side, crouched in the flower bed, and dove into the grass behind their deck. Larry's poop area, Zak thought. Not a good spot. The man, who wore a light gray work shirt, dark blue pants, and black work boots, then scrambled up the deck stairs, opened the gate, pushed aside a chair, crouched, looked furtively around, and shuffled toward the back door. One long knock was followed by two quick knocks.

Zak opened the back door slowly and saw the man pressed against the wall taking large and rapid breaths. He looked up at Zak through the screen door, held out a business card, and in a low, breathless voice said, "Ben Fisher." Deep breath. "Electrician."

Larry either heard or smelled the visitor and trotted over to the door and started to bark.

"Um, hi," Zak said, pushing Larry back with the side of his

shoe. "Do you want to come inside?"

Ben Fisher swallowed a mouthful of air, breathed it out slowly, and then nodded.

Zak held Larry's collar, opened the door, and watched as the electrician slid through the opening, keeping low to the ground. Ben Fisher looked to be about 45 years old, overweight, with a moustache and large, bushy gray eyebrows. He continued to breathe heavily.

"Dad!" Zak shouted as he closed the door.

Ben Fisher handed Zak the business card. It had the image of a big electric plug and the name of the company, Ben Fisher & Son, and below that in smaller letters, Ben Fisher, Electrician.

"I don't think…anybody…saw," Ben Fisher said breathlessly.

"Okay," Zak said, not sure what to say.

Mr. Dale hurried into the kitchen, shook the electrician's dirt-and grass-stained hand, and in a low voice said, "Thanks for your trouble."

"No problem," Ben Fisher said, still out of breath. "Haven't… done that…since the Army."

Zak took another look at Ben Fisher. Army? He didn't look like a soldier. He was old and out of shape and about as tall as Zak. He looked like a regular person, like…himself in thirty years.

Ben Fisher sniffed the air, then looked down at his shirtfront.

"Minefield…out there," he said, gesturing toward the backyard.

"Sorry," Mr. Dale said. "Our dog. We should have picked that up."

Larry looked up when he heard the word "dog."

"Where are you parked?" Mr. Dale asked.

"School lot. Two blocks south," Ben Fisher said in his deep voice, pointing with a bouncing index finger in the direction of the elementary school.

"Perfect."

"You said electrical problem. Need help. Keep it secret."

"No power since yesterday," Mr. Dale said. "Just went out on us. And my neighbor's an electrician, so I want to keep this under the radar."

"You check the circuit breakers?"

Mr. Dale nodded.

"Let's do it," Ben Fisher said, wiping his feet on the doormat.

"It's this way," Mr. Dale said, leading Ben Fisher down to the basement. Larry lost interest and walked back to the living room. Zak made a peanut butter sandwich. A short time later Mr. Dale came back up the stairs.

"He seems all right," Mr. Dale said.

"He doesn't hum," Zak said. "And I couldn't see his underwear."

"And he's not drinking our beer or watching TV, either," Mr. Dale said.

"He does smell like poop," Zak said, grinning.

"One of us should have cleaned up the backyard."

"Sorry," Zak said, his grin disappearing.

About fifteen minutes later the lights went on and Zak heard the refrigerator start up.

"Wow. That was fast," Zak said.

"Mark never fixed it that fast," Mr. Dale said.

After a few more minutes, Ben Fisher climbed up the stairs carrying the canvas bag. He paused to take a couple of breaths when he reached the top.

"You fixed it?" Mr. Dale asked.

"Fuse," Ben Fisher said. "There were a couple of replacements down there kind of tucked away."

"A fuse? I thought I had circuit breakers."

"Circuit breakers, yes," he said. "And a fused service disconnect. That was the problem."

"So it's easy to fix?" Mr. Dale asked.

"When the fuse blows, just put in a new one." Ben Fisher handed Mr. Dale a fuse with two shiny metal ends. "Hardware store probably has them."

"And that's it?"

"I checked for loose connections," Ben Fisher said. "No short circuits. No ground faults," he said. "Your real problem is an overloaded circuit."

"But you fixed it," Mr. Dale said uncertainly.

"It works, if that's what you mean," he said. "Me? I'd upgrade the service and balance the load. Be a lot safer. Your system wasn't built for these microwaves and hair dryers."

"Can you do that? I mean, fix it like you said?"

"Not now," Ben Fisher said. "I'll get my son Doug over here to help. I can schedule you for next week."

"Okay," Mr. Dale said. "And you can bring everything in through the backyard?"

"Piece of cake," Ben Fisher said.

17

The Game

Aurora stormed into the library and threw her books onto the table. Miles and Zak sat straight in their chairs. Mrs. Kaufman, helping someone at a computer workstation, gave the three of them the evil eye.

"I'm amazed, simply amazed. The way I hear it, Z, is that you're—what's the right word?—involved, I guess you could say, with that Holmes girl. Is that right? Don't tell me. I don't want to know. I mean, didn't I explain things to you? Did you listen? Apparently not. Word around the school is that you two are 'an item.' I told people they were crazy. 'Blah,' I told them. 'Blah.' It pretty much sums it up, don't you think? I have shown amazing self-control in not going directly to that girl, sitting her down, and explaining everything I know about you. No offense, Z, but you have to see it from everyone else's perspective. This is not right. The universe is out of sync."

"This has really gotten to you, hasn't it?" Miles asked, surprised.

"It's rocked my world, if you want to know," she said. "I go

95

through life with everything making sense. Then this comes along. Crash. Like glass shattering."

"You're being overdramatic," Zak said.

"She has no pores!" Aurora said. "No pores!"

"Can't you just feel good for Z? He's a nice guy."

She looked at Miles then turned to look at Zak.

"Mia and I are friends, okay?" Zak said. "She helped me out when I was cleaning the science room. We're in the same history class. We got to talking. That's it. She's really nice." He paused. "Oh, and I was over at her house last night watching a movie."

"It makes me so mad," Aurora said. "You and that blondie... it's just not right."

"It's really none of your business," Zak said.

"It's everybody's business."

"What does that mean?" Zak asked.

"You don't get it, do you?"

Zak shook his head.

"There's a whole social status world out there that you've never been a part of," she said. "You probably don't even know it exists. People talk. People scheme. It's not pretty."

"You lost me already," Zak said.

"When you're in the game, you're in the game," she said. "Blondie doesn't have a choice. With her looks, it's automatic."

"Her name's Mia," Zak said.

"Consider this a warning, Z," Aurora said. "I don't want you to get hurt."

"You have a funny way of showing it," Zak said.

Aurora picked up her books and left, her feet stomping on the gray carpet.

"Z, I hate to say this," Miles said, shaking his head. "I think Aurora likes you."

18

Loser Table

Lunchtime.

Zak sat in the school cafeteria eating a tuna salad sandwich. Every table was alive with activity and laughter and conversation—except one. His table. The loser table. Zak always sat at the loser table because it insulated him from the rest of the world. Miles, Aurora, and Mia had different lunch schedules, and everyone else in his lunch had their own groups, so he ate by himself. There were others at the table, of course, but they kept to themselves just like Zak. Pete Gentry was a thin, long-necked mainstreamed kid with autism who sat on the opposite end of the table. Zak had once been Pete's partner in biology class and both managed to get a B without saying a word to each other. Mika Nakagawa was an exchange student from Japan who ate shredded carrots and some odd-looking vegetables from her neatly-packed lunch bag. Zak had once asked her about a strange-looking piece of food, but she quickly pulled it away and started yelling at him in Japanese. That was the end of that. Violet Granderson was a large, pimply-faced girl who ate hot lunch and never made eye contact with anybody. Zak always said, "Hi, Violet" when he sat down, but the conversation ended there.

Zak was happy at the loser table. He never paid attention to what was going on in the cafeteria—the noise and the laughter and the whispers and the music and the occasional piece of food or garbage that was thrown his way. As he turned a page in #5 of Urasawa's *Pluto*, Zak took another bite of his sandwich and uncharacteristically looked over at a nearby table. He saw that it was overflowing with football and basketball players and pretty girls. Aurora was right, he thought. Mia Holmes would fit right in with that group. She had the look—the figure, the hair, the white teeth, the perfect complexion. The girls wore white or pink tops. The boys were big and muscular and wore jeans and T-shirts. Several wore maroon and white letter jackets.

As he returned to his sandwich, Zak could hear a mix of talk from the other table. He found himself listening, trying to follow along. Something about practice—basketball, probably, but it might have been swimming or cross-country. Prom. Somebody was saying something about prom. When was that? Mia was helping with the posters, so it must be in the next few weeks. But that was for juniors and seniors unless you were asked. Zak couldn't think of anything worse: music he didn't like, people he didn't like, dressing up which he didn't like. He listened to some talk about hair and clothes and a party at someone's house. Nothing he cared about. Then he thought he heard Mia's name. That got his attention. Who at that table would know Mia? Zak squinted as he looked from face to face.

"What are you looking at?" a senior girl said sharply.

The last comment silenced the table. Zak's mouth fell open and a wheat bread crumb rolled off his tongue and onto his lap. He didn't know what to say or do so he kept looking from one face to the next.

"Ignore him," one boy said, shaking his head from side to side.

"He ain't all there," said another.

They laughed.

"What?" Zak said, bewildered.

"Eat your little sandwich and read your little cartoons."

"Was he really listening?" a girl's voice whispered.

"Who is he?"

"I don't know."

"He's a loser."

Zak, red-faced and shaking, self-consciously finished his sandwich, grabbed his books and backpack, and left the cafeteria.

19

The Holy Grail

Zak and Miles sat on the floor of Miles' small bedroom. Books were everywhere, stacked in corners and on shelves, spilling out of the closet. A blue and white Danelectro guitar leaned against a chair. A microscope perched precariously on a desk next to a computer. A Talking Heads poster was taped to one eggshell-colored wall. An Xbox lay on its side. The floor was littered with dozens of opened bags of potato chips, corn chips, tortilla chips, popcorn, pretzels, pork rinds, and cheese puffs. The room had a musty, salty, greasy smell.

"I decided to do my report on the brain," Zak said as he looked into a bag of potato chips, pulled out a few, and stuffed them into his mouth.

Miles nodded but kept doodling. He'd filled an entire page with cartoons of penguins, palm trees, circles, and abstract designs.

"You hear me?"

"I'm listening. You're doing the brain." Miles put his pen down, pushed the paper away, and looked up. "Remember that you need to impress Fletcher."

"Yeah, I know," Zak said. "You got a cold? You sound like it."

"Something like that," Miles said, waving him off. "Instead of doing your report on the brain, Z, you gotta jazz it up."

"That's what I was thinking," Zak said. "So I'm actually calling it neurobiology."

"Now you're talking."

Miles loudly crunched a tortilla chip between his teeth.

"Except I probably need to add something about dentistry to get Fletcher's attention," Zak said.

"What have you got so far?" Miles asked. "That's not tooth related, that is."

"Just some notes," Zak said. "The, ah, cerebrum is the biggest part of the brain, also called the cerebral cortex. It's made of nerve cells. And there's a left and a right brain, which are called hemispheres. And each hemisphere is made of four parts...frontal lobe, parietal lobe, temporal lobe, and occipital lobe."

"Uh-huh."

"Tell me something," Zak said, pausing. "Is it me or is this really boring?"

"I can't tell. I'm falling asleep," Miles said, pretending to snore.

"There's so much here. Nerve cells called neurons—like a hundred billion of those. Dendrites, axons, synapses, gray matter, white matter, fissures, cerebellum." He sifted through his stacks of papers. "That's way too much. Nobody cares. I don't even care."

"Where's the fun stuff?"

"Well, elephant brains are bigger than human brains," Zak said. "And elephants can recognize themselves in a mirror."

"Cool," Miles said. "Got anything that isn't about elephants?"

"There's gorillas and chimps that can use sign language. And pigs and dolphins are pretty smart."

"Good."

"And I read something about cuttlefish," Zak said, paging through his notes. "They can change color and communicate."

"Sounds like you got the animal kingdom covered. But what about people? Cuttlefish and elephants are all cute and fuzzy and everything—well, maybe not all that cute or fuzzy—but people want to hear about people."

"Albert Einstein's brain is in a jar someplace. Or it was. It was cut up into more than 200 pieces."

Zak thought about the sheep's brain that had been sitting in a jar on a shelf in the science room for years. He found it incredibly depressing.

"That's good," Miles said. "Just add something about dentistry and you're there."

"How about you? How's the junk food coming?" Zak asked, looking around the room.

"Carbohydrates, fats, and salt. That's what it's all about," Miles said, spreading his notes in front of him and leaning forward animatedly. "There's like a magic number for saltiness. According to my research," Miles gestured to the open bags on the floor, "and feel free to assist at any time," Miles crunched a corn chip between his front teeth, "the optimum amount of salt in salty snack foods is in the 1.25 to 1.75 percent range. That's fairly consistent."

"Is that important?"

"It is to snack food manufacturers. It's what people crave," Miles said. "Salt is sodium chloride, which, as you know, is Na and Cl on your periodic table."

"Thanks for reminding me," Zak said, grabbing a cheese ball and tossing it at Miles.

"Thought you'd like that," Miles said, holding back a smile. "Salt keeps you in balance. In fact, there's about nine ounces of salt in the human body. That's quite a bit. It's in all your fluids… tears, sweat, blood, and mucus." Miles sneezed. "Salt helps transmit electrical impulses so your muscles can flex, your heart can beat, and your brain can think."

"Maybe I can use that brain part," Zak said. "Get some synergy going between our speeches."

"Possibly." Miles rubbed his chin thoughtfully. "Look, everybody needs salt to stay alive. But since our bodies don't make it, the only way we can get salt is to eat or drink it. So we crave salt to stay alive. Scientists have found that we also crave salt when we're thirsty or nervous or bored. We also crave salt if we need certain minerals in our diet like iron. Think about pregnant women craving pickles."

"I don't want to think about that at all."

"It's just an example."

"You have a lot on salt," Zak said.

"There's more. Carbs and oils. And proteins. I've been looking at those numbers, too. There's a pattern." Miles wiped his nose on his sleeve. "Salty snack foods are about twenty-five to thirty-five percent fat. Give or take. Fifty-five to sixty-five percent carbohydrates. And seven percent protein."

"You're losing me," Zak said.

"Z, I think I found something here," he said excitedly. "There's like a Holy Grail of junk food. A pattern they all follow. A constant. It's not just guesswork. There's a reason. An ideal. I think I got it."

"You have to be kidding."

"Maybe. But that's what I'm working on."

"The reason for junk food," Zak said, unconvinced.

"The Holy Grail," Miles said.

20

Night Creature

Zak woke to the sound of a freight train screaming through the night. He sat up, breathing quickly. He checked the time: 2:19. At least four hours before he had to get ready for school. He lay back and listened. Metal on metal. A long whistle and then two bursts. What was it saying? What was it trying to tell him? He closed his eyes and imagined the powerful engine dragging a line of dull freight cars along the metal track, scraping and sparking and rocking across the countryside like some prehistoric beast. The train had an elemental purpose, moving in a direction. What was his purpose? What direction was he going? Zak had never thought about his place in the universe. He was alive and doing what was expected of him: going to school, attending church, hanging out with friends, being with his family. That was life. Now it seemed that there was more—more to do and more that was expected of him. It was a strange feeling. He was excited, but he was also afraid. Zak lay in bed and wrestled with the creature of the night.

21

Variables

"Z! Z!" a voice shouted from behind Zak as he walked through the crowded high school hallway. Zak was just leaving the science room and heading for his math class. Final period. Mrs. Yeager.

Zak glanced behind him and slowed as he saw Mia Holmes striding up quickly. She wore pink running shoes, short jeans, a pink top, and a jean jacket. She also carried a purse, books, and a large rolled up piece of paper. Zak gave her a big smile.

"Mia. Hi," Zak said, stepping out of the traffic to stand next to a stainless steel drinking fountain with yellow and green chewing gum blocking the drain holes.

"I want to show you something," she said, jostled by someone passing through the hallway. "Take a look at this."

Mia held out the tube of paper. Zak looked at Mia, unrolled it, and saw two posters with fancy borders. One had a black and white picture of Abraham Lincoln with his beard and mole and the word "Important!" The other had a black and white photo of a plain-looking woman in a fancy black dress. Her lips were thin, showing neither frown nor smile, but giving the impression of impatience. Her hair was parted in the middle and pulled tight against her skull with a black headband; several curls rested on her left shoulder. Zak looked at Mia and then back at the poster. Zak unrolled it all the way to reveal a single word: "Trivia!"

"Mary Todd Lincoln?" Zak asked, looking at Mia and laughing.

"Uh-huh." Mia laughed showing her perfect imperfect teeth.

"This is amazing. You're a real artist," Zak said. A fancy multi-colored border surrounded each of the photos and the words stood out against the background. "You gonna give them to Mr. Brown?"

Mia shook her head.

"I thought we could sneak them into his room when he's not there," she said. "After all, we're pretty good with all that stealth stuff."

Zak nodded, then turned his head to look up and down the hallway, which was unusually quiet. Mia looked around, too.

"How about we meet here after school," Zak said quickly, rolling up the posters and handing them to Mia like a baton in a relay race.

"Perfect," Mia said.

"See you then."

"See you."

They took off in different directions, moving fast. Zak turned the corner, passed the first door, then turned left into the second door, and slid into his desk chair just as the bell rang. He was sweating hard.

Mrs. Yeager, a stout woman with snow-white hair and glasses, stood at the front of the classroom. On her chin was a small scar that, she explained to her classes, was shaped like an irregular convex pentagon. Twenty solutions were projected onto a screen

106

behind her.

"Exchange assignments, check them against the answers on the screen, and return them to your partner. Are there any questions?"

After a few minutes of papers shuffling back and forth the room was filled with an end-of-the-day silence.

"We will now dive a little deeper into factoring—factoring trinomials," she said. "Who can tell me what a trinomial is?"

Silence.

"Anybody?"

Silence.

"Then I will explain." She turned to the whiteboard and wrote $x^2 + 2x + 1$. "X squared plus two x plus one. This is an example of a trinomial. You see the three terms...x^2 and 2x and 1...tri means three. A binomial has two terms and trinomial has three. Any questions?"

Zak stared at the whiteboard but he didn't see it. He glanced around and saw that the rest of the class was sleeping, texting, or daydreaming. Nobody took notes or looked at a textbook.

"The idea of factoring is to find the roots of an equation. In this case, we want to find the two binomials that, when multiplied together, will result in this trinomial. Questions?"

None.

"It may seem difficult at first, but let me show you the answer and we will work it through together and have a better idea how to factor." She wrote "(x + 1)" and "(x + 1)" beside each other on the whiteboard. "When you multiply two binomials together, you multiply the first term in the first binomial by the first term in the second binomial—x times x is x squared." She wrote x^2 on the whiteboard. "Then multiply the second term in the first binomial by the first term in the second binomial." She wrote 1x on the

107

whiteboard. "Questions?"

Mrs. Yeager was about to proceed but was startled by a voice from the back of the classroom.

"I have a question."

It was a girl's voice. Zak and the rest of the class turned to look. Trudy Taylor from his American History class had her hand raised. Trudy never said anything unless called upon, and even then she was mousy and hard to hear. This made Zak take notice.

"Yes," Mrs. Yeager said, adjusting her glasses. "What is your question?"

"Is this important?" Trudy Taylor asked. Her voice broke, but she was still loud enough to hear.

"Is what important?" Mrs. Yeager asked.

"This…factoring," Trudy Taylor said.

"You will need to know it for your next test, if that is what you mean."

"I guess I mean," Trudy Taylor said, uncertainly, "will we use this in life?"

"Yeah, why study all this?" James Dealey asked.

"We're never gonna use it," Tami Westerberg said.

"It seems like such a waste of time," Edward Perez added.

This was the most activity Zak ever remembered in Mrs. Yeager's class. It must be because the school year was nearly over, Zak thought. Or maybe Mr. Brown was having an effect on people.

"Quiet, quiet," Mrs. Yeager said, and then added a little more forcefully, "I need quiet, please."

The class quieted down.

"Thank you." Mrs. Yeager looked around the room. "This is not the first class to ask that question. When we get beyond simple addition, subtraction, multiplication, and division—especially as we work our way through algebra and into calculus—the reason isn't all that clear."

Trudy Taylor and most of the class nodded silently.

"Many people ask, 'When am I going to use this?' and 'What good is algebra?'"

Mrs. Yeager moved away from her spot at the front of the classroom. She never did that. The class collectively sat up straight.

"Tell me, in what job do you read stories as you do in your English classes? In what job do you observe caterpillars as you do in your science classes? Why would any person need to know who killed the Archduke Franz Ferdinand? Unless you're a teacher or a specialist, that is. Tell me."

Edward Perez shook his head.

"Anybody?"

Everyone shook their heads.

"Mathematics teaches you to solve problems," Mrs. Yeager said firmly. "Let me repeat that. Mathematics teaches you to solve problems." She switched off the projector. "And that is one thing I can assure you that you will have when you grow up: problems."

Out of the corner of his eye Zak saw Trudy open her textbook.

"Mathematics exercises the mind. It will help you improve your critical thinking, structure your thoughts, boost your creativity, and help you to solve problems. Can any other class say as much?"

Silence.

"A good question, Miss," Mrs. Yeager said. "Now we move on."

Mrs. Yeager continued to explain factoring, which started to make sense to Zak. He'd never thought of math as anything more than a class he had to take. In life, people were always faced with problems that they struggled to find answers for, or some kind of truth. There were lots of problems, but the solutions, if you could call them that, were messy and complicated. Could men and women be reduced to some kind of formula like x plus y? Could he? Z. His name was a variable. An unknown. Somehow that didn't make him feel better.

22

Gone Missing

Mrs. Dale hung up the phone.

"What?" Mr. Dale said. "What's wrong?"

"Grandma's...gone," Mrs. Dale said haltingly, her face drained of color.

"She's dead?" Zak asked.

"Grandma died?" Chloe said.

"No, no. She's not dead," Mrs. Dale said quickly. "She's just...not where she's supposed to be."

Mrs. Dale lowered herself onto the sofa and stared at the blank wall across the living room. Zak had never seen his mother like this. Normally she was in control of her emotions, but now she seemed suddenly adrift. It made him nervous.

"Who was that on the phone?" Mr. Dale said. He sat down on the sofa next to his wife and gently placed his hand on her shoulder.

"Ms. Casper from Green Valley," Mrs. Dale said listlessly. "They were doing a regular check and didn't get an answer. They went into the room but she's not there. Not anywhere."

"What does that mean?" Chloe said. "Is she dead or isn't she dead?"

"Shhhh," Mr. Dale said. "She isn't dead."

"How do you know?" Chloe asked stubbornly.

"Just be quiet, dear," Mr. Dale said.

"Both she and Mrs. Ramsey are gone," Mrs. Dale said.

An emptiness filled the room. Nobody knew what to say or think. Zak wondered if he would ever see his grandmother again. That scared him. He thought about their last visit, how secretive she seemed, Mrs. Ramsey's envelope, and the red Mustang convertible in the parking lot. Then it suddenly made sense.

"Road trip," Zak said, nodding his head and smiling.

"What?" Mr. Dale said, confused.

"Mother wouldn't do that," Mrs. Dale said. "She's 82."

"What does age have to do with it?" Zak asked.

Zak was sure of it. All the pieces fit together. The car, the whispers, the need to get away from Green Valley. It was all there.

"We can call the police," Mr. Dale said. "Or maybe they did that already."

"No," Mrs. Dale said, turning to look at her husband. "We were the first call. Ms. Casper wondered if we knew something. I told her I'd call her back once we talk it over."

"Grandma can look after herself," Zak said. Then he added, "Can't she?"

After Zak's grandfather had died, Grandma Morris had been lonely and confused. When she moved to Green Valley from the house she had lived in for more than 50 years, she seemed changed. It was like she was a ghost just taking up space, passing through the hours like passing through walls. Life didn't hold anything new or exciting.

"She's not like she was," Mrs. Dale said. "After Grandfather

Morris died. And that fall she took."

"There's no telling where she might be if she's with that new friend of hers," Mr. Dale said.

"I like Mrs. Miriam Harriet Truth Ramsey," Chloe said.

"We do too," agreed Mr. Dale. "It's just that…she might have been putting ideas into your grandmother's head."

"You act like she's an escaped prisoner," Zak said.

"I'm just worried," Mrs. Dale said. "She would have called. Or told us…something."

"So you'd tell her she's crazy and can't go?" Zak said.

"This is your grandmother we're talking about," Mr. Dale said sharply to Zak. "She's not in the habit of disappearing."

"All I'm saying is that I don't want to be a prisoner when I'm 82," Zak said.

"I didn't know Grandma was a prisoner," Chloe said. "What did she do?"

"She got old," Zak said.

"Zak, please be quiet," Mr. Dale said firmly. "Think of your mother. This is a serious matter."

Zak was serious, but nothing he said mattered. After all, he was just a kid. And his grandmother…what she wanted didn't matter, either. She was old. It was like there was only one opinion that mattered.

"She and Mrs. Ramsey checked out at the front desk," Mrs. Dale said. "That was yesterday. They seemed all cheerful. Said they were going to the store."

"Maybe they just got turned around," Mr. Dale said.

"Oh, dear," Mrs. Dale said. "Her medicine. I hope she has her medicine."

"Susan, I think we should go over to Green Valley and talk to Ms. Casper and take a look at the apartment. I'm sure there's an explanation. I'm sure we'll find her."

"Yes. You're right, you're right," Mrs. Dale said distractedly.

Zak was sure Grandma Morris and her friend were out driving somewhere, maybe taking a real road trip hundreds or even thousands of miles away. Life was full of dangers and risks. His grandmother knew that. But even more important, she needed to get away. Away from the life that wasn't a life any more. Zak hoped he had his grandmother's courage.

Mr. Dale turned to Zak and Chloe. "You two can stay here. Zak, you're in charge. Take care of your sister. And be sure to let Larry out while we're gone."

Zak nodded.

"Are we ever going to see Grandma again?" Chloe asked nervously.

Mrs. Dale bent down and kissed her daughter on the forehead.

"We'll find her," Mrs. Dale said, her eyes tearing up. "Grandma Morris can take care of herself."

Chloe's eyes lit up.

"I can't wait to tell my friends that my grandma escaped from prison," Chloe said.

23

A Question

The library was busier than usual during fourth period. An English class had been let loose to do research and the students were spread out among the many computer workstations and logged onto their Facebook pages. Zak and Miles sat at a distant table, separate from everything and everyone.

"I got a question, Miles," Zak said.

A sophomore boy passed close by and Zak waited until he was gone.

"There's this girl...," Zak said.

"Mia Holmes," Miles said.

"What?"

"You're talking about Mia Holmes."

"How do you know that?"

"Z, how many girls do you know? Your mom, your sister, your grandmother, Aurora, and Mia Holmes. That's it. I'm guessing you're not asking about your mom, grandmother, or sister. And Aurora...there's no understanding her. Nobody tries. It's like looking into the sun—you just don't do it. That leaves one person."

"You're right," Zak said shaking his head. "So what do you think about what Aurora said? I mean, that I should stay away."

"You can't take what Aurora says seriously," Miles said, pushing a *Popular Science* magazine toward the center of the table. "You should know that by now."

"But she's right," Zak said, fidgeting with a dull pencil that was about two inches long. "Mia is popular and I'm...not. You even said as much."

"It's not about being popular. That's not important. Be yourself. Don't worry about what other people think. And don't sell yourself short."

Zak looked at Miles and sighed.

"At lunch the other day I was looking at a table with a lot of the popular juniors and seniors," Zak said. "Mia could fit right in. Me, I sit at the loser table with Violet Granderson."

"I thought Violet transferred," Miles said.

Zak shook his head. "Nope. Still here. Still doesn't say a word."

"All I can say is, don't be like Violet Granderson," Miles said.

"That's it? That's your advice?" Zak said. "What if Mia wants to do something? It's not like I have money or a car or anything."

"Talk to her," Miles said. "Or ask her to shoot hoops with us."

"Really?"

"I'm joking, Z."

"I'm just looking for an idea."

"If it happens, make something up," Miles said. "You're good at that."

"You're not much help."

"If she likes you, it shouldn't really matter what you do. Or what other people think."

24

Secrets

Zak stood awkwardly in front of his locker and watched the school empty. He was near the end of a bank of lockers not far from the main entrance. Metal doors slammed, voices rose, laughter intensified, and students moved urgently toward the exits. There was a sense of excitement and renewal. After a few minutes, Mia arrived breathless and smiling. Zak had asked her to meet him after her last class.

"Sorry it took so long," she said. "My locker is way on the other side of school."

"I'm surprised you even got a locker," Zak said.

"I think some kid must have died in there," she said. "It certainly smells like it. It's hideous!"

They laughed.

"I was just past Mr. Brown's room," Zak said, fishing for something to say. "Those posters look great."

"Thanks for helping," Mia said. "I hope he's not mad."

"Why would he be mad?"

"We did it without his permission," she said. "He might feel violated or something."

"He'll love them," Zak said. "You're good at art."

They walked together through the main doors to the front yard and stepped into the grass underneath the broad branches of the Adams Oak, the tall, welcoming tree that was the symbol for the school. Zak looked around, not sure what to say or do. Streams of people passed by.

"So, do you want to do something?" Mia asked uncertainly.

"Um," Zak said. "I…I was going to go over to Miles' house and shoot baskets."

Zak cursed himself for not being able to think of anything better.

"Oh. Okay," she said. Mia's head tilted a little to the side as if she wanted to say something else.

"You can come," Zak said quickly, desperately. "Miles won't mind."

"Really?"

"It's not like we do anything. We just hang out."

"If you think it's okay," Mia said.

"Sure." Zak waved his hand dismissively. "He won't have a problem. You'll like Miles."

As they walked along the sidewalk, both Zak and Mia looked up at the sky. High above, a white egret circled lazily.

"Do you know what you want to do, Z?" Mia asked. "With your life?"

"I haven't thought about it much," Zak said slowly. "Maybe psychology. Or the Army. Find some way to help people."

Mia Holmes nodded.

"How about you?" he asked, glancing at Mia's face.

"Maybe a lawyer. I'm not really sure, either."

"My dad's always telling me I have lots of time to decide.

That it's important to be a kid," Zak said.

"I'm not sure I know what it's like to be a kid any more. It's like I'm stuck somewhere in the middle," Mia said.

They crossed the street, running to avoid a speeding driver.

"Do you ever get the feeling you won't make it as an adult?" Mia asked as they reached the other side of the street.

"I know, I know," Zak said hurriedly. "I thought it was just me."

"It kind of scares me. But then I look around at the world and all the problems...and I think—I know—I can do better. Because I care," she said. "It's just that, what I'm afraid of is not caring. You know what I mean?" Mia said.

"I suppose. But I'm not sure I know what's really important," Zak said.

"My dad says I think everything is important," Mia said.

Zak pointed ahead.

"That's Miles in the driveway two houses down."

Miles was shooting baskets: spinning, jumping, and occasionally getting the ball to fall into the hoop.

"Did you try out for the team?" Mia asked.

"The school team?" Zak laughed. "Neither of us is any good. And with my size, I haven't got a chance. Everybody's over six feet tall. And Miles is a geek. It's just fun. We talk."

They came to the driveway and watched Miles miss an easy layup.

"That was embarrassing," Zak shouted.

Miles turned, smiled, and saluted.

"I didn't know I had an audience," he said, picking up the ball and walking toward Zak and Mia.

"Miles," Zak said. "This is Mia. Mia Holmes."

Miles looked at his dirty hand, held it back, and gave Mia a little wave from the hip.

"Hi," he said.

"Hi. Nice to finally meet you, Miles. Z talks a lot about you."

"Mia wasn't doing anything and I said she could hang out with us," Zak said.

Miles rolled his eyes at Zak.

"If it's okay," Mia said quickly.

"Yeah. No problem. As you can tell, I'm not very good. Every once in a while I can even make a basket," Miles said in a nasal voice.

"You still got that cold?" Zak asked.

"Just stuffed up," he said, shrugging his shoulders.

Zak and Mia set their books and bags in the grass and joined Miles in the middle of the driveway. Miles tossed the ball to Zak who made a fake to his right and then a jump shot that hit the rim and bounced over to Mia's feet. She bent down, picked up the ball, and looked at the backboard.

"You don't have to play if you don't want to," Zak said.

Mia jumped and effortlessly launched the ball through the air. It fell silently through the basket.

"Wow," Zak said.

"That's unbelievable," Miles said. "Where'd you learn to do that?"

"I played on a traveling team. Back in Wisconsin."

"We're out of our league," Miles said.

"You must think we're losers," Zak said.

"This is what basketball should be," she said. "I've been playing since first grade. I like it, but it's not fun any more. Competitive basketball, I mean. But I still like shooting like this."

"You should go out for the team," Miles said. "I mean, talent like yours…"

"You should talk," Zak said to Miles. "You don't do anything with your talent. You don't care about anything."

"I take offense at that," Miles said, picking up the ball and tossing it to Zak. "I care about not caring."

"Miles is like a genius," Zak said to Mia. "He's probably the smartest kid in our class. But even I get better grades sometimes."

"Probably? Probably the smartest?" Miles said. "Z, I'm offended."

"My mom says grades aren't that important," Mia said. "Of course, my dad grounds me when I get a B."

"It seems like there's all this pressure to get good grades but nobody cares if we learn anything," Zak said. "Even some of the teachers."

"There's a few that are okay," Miles said.

"Yeah, like Mr. Brown," Mia said.

"What's the deal with Brown? There's some who say he walks on water, and others want him run out of town," Miles said.

"Really? I hadn't heard…," Zak said, and then stopped to think. "The other day I saw him erasing something on the whiteboard. A stick figure hanging on a noose. Like a lynching."

Miles shook his head.

"That's horrible. I don't know why anybody would do that," Mia said. "He's a great teacher. He gets everyone interested." Mia added, "And Z here knows everything."

"Z?" Miles asked, stealing the ball out of Zak's hands. "This Z?"

"Yeah, well, he's a good teacher," Zak said.

"Z knows all the answers. Mr. Brown always asks him the tough questions," Mia said.

"He teaches differently," Zak said. "Like at the start of every class he goes through the same questions. It's like, 'Who is Benjamin Franklin? Who is Thomas Jefferson? Who is James Madison? Who is Thomas Paine? Who is George Washington? Who is John Adams? Who is Alexander Hamilton?' Rapid fire like that. It started that way and someone would answer, 'Thomas Paine wrote "Common Sense."' And the next day it's, 'Thomas Paine wrote "Common Sense"' and 'he's a famous journalist' and 'he hated King George the Third' and 'he got people excited about the revolution.'"

"And that's just the first five minutes," Mia said.

"Patrick Henry," Zak said.

"'Give me liberty or give me death!'" Mia responded.

"Give me the basketball and let me shoot," Miles said. He turned to the basket and put up an air ball. He shrugged his shoulders, sighed, turned to Mia, and said, "So what's up with you?"

"Huh?" Mia asked suspiciously. "What do you mean?"

"You're like some mystery woman. You come in here out of the blue with only about a month left of school. You're this basketball star."

"I'm not a star," Mia said.

"Whatever," Miles said. "Aurora thinks you're some kind of mobster. What gives?"

Mia shrugged her shoulders. "My dad got a job here. We moved nearby and this is where I have to go to school."

"I still think there's some mystery," Miles said.

"Don't mind him, Mia. He's just playing with you," Zak said.

"Everybody has secrets," Mia said. "I bet you have secrets, Miles."

"Yeah," Miles said. He thought for a minute. "Tell you what. I'll tell you a secret, but then you have to tell me one of yours. You too, Z. Deal?"

122

"Okay," Mia said, nodding.

"I'll start," Miles said. "My secret is that…I like to watch pro wrestling."

"Wrestling?" Mia asked.

"With the masks and the makeup and the glitter and the throwing chairs?" Zak asked.

"I don't know why, but there you go," Miles said. "You can make fun of me if you want. That's my secret. Your turn."

"I don't really have any secrets," Zak said. "Not like that. Um, I like comic books. And some manga. Maybe that's my secret."

"It's not much of a secret," Mia said. "Your T-shirts are all Spider-Man and Batman and Swamp Thing."

"Here's a secret about Z," Miles said to Mia. "He's a poet."

"Miles," Zak said.

"Last year he wrote the best poem in the class."

"I want to hear it." Mia clapped her hands together.

"It's really not that great. And it doesn't rhyme."

"Do you know it by heart?" Mia said.

"It's not very long." Zak gave in and then cleared his throat. "It's called, 'Talking to a Pigeon About Poetry.'"

"I like that," Mia said.

"Keep going, Z," Miles said.

"It's two words. It goes: 'Hi.' 'Coo.'"

Zak lowered his head, blushing. "That's all there is," he said.

"That's hilarious! I love it," Mia said, wiping a tear away from her eye. "You shouldn't keep that secret. You should get that published."

"Okay," Miles said, gesturing to Mia. "Your turn."

"I don't know," she said quietly. "You have to promise not to tell anyone." She paused and blushed. "It's a tattoo."

"Where…where is it?"

"My friends and I went to the mall one day and we were all talking about getting tattoos or piercings. Big talk. But we needed permission from a parent, so we couldn't do it." Mia paused. "Except I came back the next day with my mom."

Zak and Miles looked at Mia's arms and legs and neck.

"Is it…um…hidden?" Zak asked nervously.

"My left ankle."

Zak and Miles knelt down to look at Mia's ankle.

"I don't see it," Zak said.

"You have to look close," she said. "I wanted to get one that's just for me. One that wouldn't stand out too much. So I thought it would be cool to have a constellation made of stars that looked like freckles or moles."

"Cassiopeia," Miles said, leaning forward to get within a foot of Mia's ankle.

Mia nodded. "That's right." She pointed to the five dots—tiny suns—that formed a rough W. "That's my middle name."

"I'm impressed," Miles said.

"Hidden in plain view," Zak said. "Did it hurt?"

"Yeah," she said. "Don't believe what everyone says. Mine doesn't look like much, but it hurt for days."

"You're full of surprises," Miles said. "No wonder Z likes you."

25

Star Power

"Students? Young scientists? Take your seats?"

Dr. Cyrus B. Fletcher stood straight-backed and tall at the front of the science classroom and clapped his hands together two times to get the attention of Zak's class. It was a futile effort. Zak slouched low in his seat with his eyes open, but most of the other students buried their heads in their elbows as they tried to find comfortable sleeping positions. Zak glanced to the back of the room to see if anybody was paying attention. As he did, he locked eyes with Felix the armadillo. It felt like the armadillo was watching over him and at the same time challenging him to be better or different. Zak found it disturbing. He turned back and sat up straight just as Dr. Fletcher fixed him with an anxious glance.

"Young ladies and young gentlemen?" Dr. Fletcher said loudly, tapping a pen on his desk. "I want to remind you that topics and outlines for your presentations are due this week. I also have a sign-up schedule for the preliminary rounds, where we will select the finalists."

"I thought we didn't have to do it," Heidi Miller called out.

"Miss Miller? Yes?" Dr. Fletcher located Heidi Miller's long, sharp-featured face and brown eyes, glanced down at his notes, then back up. "It is not a requirement, but I hope you will consider it? I am calling our scientific get-together the John Quincy Adams Science Series. It is open to all freshmen, as you know. All freshmen. I have enlisted the help of scientific experts from outside the school, and I am arranging for a prize to be awarded to the winner."

"Prize? What sort of prize?" asked Julius Hernandez, a cross-country runner with a slight lisp.

"I have spoken to several local establishments, and I am—how shall I say?—hopeful. Nothing firm yet, of course. Stay tuned." Dr. Fletcher looked from student to student. "As I have mentioned many times, your presentation must be about 'Science in the Real World.' Are we clear on that?"

No response.

"Very well. Our lesson today is about chemical elements," Dr. Fletcher began, turning off the lights and projecting an image onto the screen from his computer. The two words "Chemical Elements" appeared in orange and black letters.

Zak was ready to fall asleep. Dr. Fletcher's voice and bulleted lists caused him to lose focus quickly. He wondered if he could write a speech good enough to win the prize. Probably not. Especially if Miles and Kim Sather were competing, too. Miles could win it. Zak wouldn't mind losing to Miles. But if Kim Sather won, that would put her in the lead for the summer science job, even after Zak had cleaned the room. He didn't want that to happen.

"I trust that you have not forgotten the periodic table of the elements?" Dr. Fletcher gestured to the large poster that hung on the wall. "I have not yet made it through all the examinations, but so far I am—how shall I say it?—pleasantly surprised? Yes?" The teacher seemed to look right at Zak.

Zak found Fletcher's lessons freakishly compelling, like watching a car crash in slow motion. His own involuntary attentiveness during class was probably one of the reasons Fletcher had singled him out and asked him to clean the science lab. What seemed like profound interest and a love of science was actually an inability to look away. He watched Fletcher pace back and forth at the front of the room, occasionally grasping the lapels of his sport coat, tugging at his vest, or stopping and staring at the class with his fish eyes. Zak had always figured that Fletcher would trip over a stool, swallow his tongue, or fall on the floor in some extraordinary fit of palsy. He didn't want to miss it when it happened.

The image on the screen changed to a bullet pointed list.

"All matter is made up of elements—chemical elements—which are made of atoms. An element is in its simplest form. It cannot be split up or changed into another substance," Dr. Fletcher droned. "Elements can be gasses, solids, or liquids."

Dr. Fletcher stopped and looked around the classroom, his nostrils flaring. He flashed a smile, showing his perfect teeth.

"Elements are everyday things like hydrogen, oxygen, iron, silver, and gold," he continued. "There are also some exotic elements that have been created in laboratories. Like Fermium… Fm…number 100 on the table…Seaborgium…Sg…number 106 on the table…Meitnerium…Mt…number 109 on the table."

Zak looked at the wrinkled, faded periodic table that hung on the side wall. He still remembered most of the elements, which made him feel good. He also thought he did pretty well on the test. It was matching, so with the tricks he and Miles worked on there were only a couple of elements he wasn't sure about.

A new list appeared on the screen.

"As an example," Fletcher continued, "the human body is made almost entirely of six elements: oxygen, carbon, hydrogen, nitrogen, calcium, and phosphorous."

Six elements? Zak found that amazing. By putting six elements together in just the right way you could make a human being. Was that even possible? Zak could barely make macaroni and cheese in a microwave oven.

"The earth itself is mostly made of oxygen, silicon, aluminum, iron, calcium, sodium, potassium, and magnesium. Eight elements," Fletcher said.

Zak wondered how an element like calcium knew it was part of a person rather than part of the earth. He also wondered if it had any choice.

"The universe?" Fletcher asked cryptically, then stopped and waited. A few heads drifted up to look at the clock on the wall and then dropped back down. Fletcher walked over to one of the windows and gestured outside. "In the universe, hydrogen makes up about 75 percent of all matter. When you add helium and oxygen, that takes care of about 99 percent of everything. In other words, in the universe, human beings are, as you might say, unique."

Zak thought about that. He liked the idea of people as special. He watched as another bulleted list appeared.

"A Russian named Dmitri Mendeleev in 1869 created the original periodic table of the elements." Mendeleev. That was the name he'd read in his textbook and that Miles had mentioned when they were studying. "His table had 65 elements, which is all that were known at the time. His table went from the lowest atomic weight to the highest atomic weight. Today's chart, which shows 118 elements, has an abbreviation of the name and the atomic *number* rather than the atomic weight. The atomic number, which is often abbreviated 'Z,' is the number of protons in the nucleus of an atom."

Z? Trudy Taylor and Fuzz Preston, who were also in Zak's science class, looked in his direction and snickered.

"If you remember back to the start of today's class," Dr. Fletcher said, "I told you that elements cannot be changed into other elements. That is not exactly true." He smiled and raised his eyebrows. Zak found it alarming. "Hundreds of years ago, alchemists were obsessed with the idea of transforming lead—a common base metal—into gold, a precious metal. That is, changing Pb or plumbum with an atomic number of 82—82 protons—into Au or aurum with an atomic number, Z, of 79—79 protons."

What was Fletcher saying? It was confusing, but there was something in there that got Zak's attention. Alchemists wanted to take something ordinary like lead and turn it into something valuable like gold. That was interesting.

"Alchemists were unsuccessful," Dr. Fletcher said. "But today's scientists have managed to do what those alchemists could not. They have turned lead to gold. They do it through the use of nuclear reactors and particle accelerators. It is a process called transmutation." Dr. Fletcher gave a forced chuckle. "Now, before you get ideas about getting rich, I'll have you know that this kind of change—removing three protons from the lead nucleus to get Z to 79—requires an incredible amount of energy. The power of a star like the sun, in fact. It is also extremely expensive. Much more than a teacher's salary or your allowance."

Turning lead into gold…was it really possible? It would be like turning a dog into a cat or an orange into a pineapple. Could things change? Could people change? Could he change? Even Zak didn't know the answer to that.

26

Invisible Man

Zak was anxious, vigilant, his eyes darting left and right. He had positioned himself just inside the doors that Mia Holmes had to go through to exit the school at the end of the day. He watched as hundreds of students passed by, chattering, laughing, and pushing as they escaped into the beautiful spring day. He knew that Mia could have slipped past him, gone through another exit, or had an after-school project or activity. Still, Zak stood, stared, waited, hoped. What he found most surprising was the number of people he didn't know. Occasionally he'd see someone from one of his classes, but mostly he saw strangers. Hundreds of strangers.

Just when he began to get discouraged, Zak saw Mia Holmes walking toward the main doors and talking with two girls he didn't know. They didn't look like freshmen. More like sophomores or juniors. One was taller than Mia, with brown hair, bright red lips, and a black Woodstock T-shirt. The other was a little smaller than Mia, but with straight black hair cut short, glasses, a white blouse, and a floral print skirt. All three were laughing and enjoying themselves, carrying large purses slung over their shoulders, and holding phones.

Zak fought to control his breathing. He'd assumed that Mia would be alone. Now what? Why did girls always travel in groups? That made him nervous. He thought about ducking down the hallway before she saw him, but instead he raised his hand in a halfhearted wave and added an equally weak, "Hi, Mia." He wasn't sure what made her turn and look in his direction, but she did. Zak could see the recognition in her eyes followed by a vigorous wave of her own. The other two girls looked at Zak and then at each other, and shook their heads disapprovingly.

"Sure you don't want a ride?" Zak heard Woodstock ask.

"I gotta go home first," Mia said to her. "I'll meet you there in 30."

"See ya, Mia," Flower Girl said.

The two girls laughed and continued to talk as they walked out of the school.

Mia skipped over to where Zak stood.

"Hey, Z," she said with a bright smile.

"Hi, Mia." He was excited to see her but didn't have the kind of outward enthusiasm she had. It was like she had some kind of power switch. He could feel the electricity.

"You headed out?" Mia asked. Zak nodded. "This was like the longest day," she said, exhaling hard. "I couldn't wait for it to end. I just want to get outside where it's warm and I don't have to think about school."

"Yeah," Zak said, holding the door open for her.

"Thanks."

They both looked up at the sky. Blue. Sun. No clouds. Perfect.

"I feel like a rat in a cage when I'm inside on a day like this," Zak said.

"When it gets to this time of the year my mind kind of checks out," Mia said. "It's hard to concentrate."

"I know what you mean," he said. "We had a test in English today. *Of Mice and Men*. It was hard to focus. And we only had, like, three or four days to read it."

They walked past the Adams Oak tree, its leaves like a thousand tiny, green, growing hands waving at them as they passed. Zak figured he'd walk home with Mia. Would she mind? He didn't know. He was always questioning himself. He thought about the two girls she'd been talking to. It kind of bothered him that she was getting to know so many people. It felt like he was being nudged out of her life a little bit every day.

"I think you know more people than I do," Zak said. "And you've only been here for a few weeks."

"I make friends easily, I guess," she said. "Like today. I'm getting together with Tina and Margo at the coffee shop. They seem real nice."

The cars in the parking lot jockeyed for position, squealing their tires, trying to get out and away. Zak remembered what Aurora had said about "the game." It seemed as if it was going on all around him and he was clueless—as if he were standing in the eye of a hurricane.

"You're lucky," Zak said.

"I think anybody can be like that if they try."

Zak shook his head. "It's who you are," he said. "And how you look."

Mia was silent for a moment and then nodded.

"You're right," she said. "But that's not always a good thing."

They crossed the street, avoiding the traffic.

"I mentioned you to some other friends," Mia said, stopping to look at Zak as they reached the curb. "They never even heard of you."

"I fly under the radar."

"You don't have to," Mia said forcefully. "Don't you want to do things and get to know more people? I need to keep busy or I get bored."

She chewed gum with her mouth open. Zak had never noticed that before.

"I do stuff," Zak said.

Zak wasn't sure what he actually did. Not much. Hanging out with Miles. Watching TV and old movies. Listening to music. Riding his bike. Video games. Computers. As he thought about it, it all seemed pointless and foolish.

"Maybe you should get out and meet more people," Mia said. "Don't you do anything like sports or anything?"

Zak shook his head.

"I ride my bike. Out in the country…it's so peaceful and you get away from the cars and just go…anywhere…and nowhere. You know what I mean? It's like being free."

"You are free," Mia said, laughing.

Zak shook his head. "I don't know about that."

As they approached Mia's home, Zak could feel a sudden change in the weather. The wind stopped blowing and the birds became quiet. He even stopped breathing for a second. It was strange.

"I'm going to prom," Mia Holmes said quickly, looking at a lawn covered with bright yellow dandelions, then at Zak.

"You are?"

"Yeah," she said. "Kevin—Kevin Rourke—asked me. He was helping with the prom posters. I think he's a junior. Do you know him?"

"He's that basketball player?"

"I guess. He seems nice and all."

Zak's body and mood slumped. Aurora was right. Mia Holmes was in a different world. Kevin Rourke was a basketball star and popular and tall and two years older and drove a car. There was no comparison. Zak couldn't compete with that. Freshmen couldn't even go to prom unless they were asked.

"Does he know you play basketball?" Zak asked, searching for something to say.

"He really doesn't know much about me," she said.

"He just asked you," Zak said quietly.

"I think it'll be fun," Mia said.

Zak had never been interested in dances or social events. He never felt comfortable in groups like that.

"You'll have a great time," Zak said unenthusiastically.

"I wish you were going, too."

"Me?" Zak said. "That's the last place I'd want to be. No offense." He reflected a moment, tilted his head, and said, "I'll just stay home and...eat ants."

"Eat ants? Is that what you said?" Mia asked, confused.

"It's a joke," Zak said, and then added, "sort of."

27

Ghosts

Nightfall.

Two shadows moved through the grass behind the Dale home: one short and wide, the other tall and thin. The shadows were accompanied by sounds: a rustle of branches, casual swearing, the muted rattle of metal and plastic.

"Shhhh," a voice said.

"Shhhh yourself," the other voice said.

Zak looked out the screen door. Chloe looked out, too.

"Are they ghosts?" Chloe asked.

"Electricians," Zak said.

"Why are they in the dark like that?"

"So the neighbors can't see them."

A big brown moth attached itself to the screen door and then flew away. Zak and Chloe continued to stare blindly into the darkness, barely able to make out two moving shapes.

"Ouch," a voice said in the night.

"I told you to bring a flashlight," the other voice said.

Zak turned on the outside light when he heard the deck gate

open. The shapes materialized into two men carrying tool bags and a large cardboard box. Both blinked furiously as their eyes tried to adjust to the light.

"Ben Fisher," the short, wide older man said.

"And son," the tall, thin younger man added. "We're here about the electricity."

The two stumbled toward the door. Moths swarmed around their heads, forming living halos. Zak held the door open and the electricians managed to get their bags and box into the kitchen. A few moths followed, fluttering around the ceiling lights inside.

"My dad will be back soon," Zak said. "He's at a church meeting."

"This is my son Doug," Ben Fisher said. As before, Ben Fisher was dressed in a light gray shirt and blue pants.

"Hi," Zak said. "I'm Zak and this is Chloe."

"I'm eight," Chloe said.

"Um, yeah, hi," Doug Fisher said uncomfortably. He towered over all of them. Probably six-five, Zak figured. He was dressed in a white T-shirt, jeans, and tennis shoes. He had a narrow face, slits for eyes, and rough stubble around his chin. A cut ran down the side of his left cheek.

"There's blood," Chloe said, pointing at a red streak on Doug Fisher's cheek.

"There's some low branches out there," Doug said. "Hard to see with all this dark."

"We'll get started," Ben Fisher said. He turned to his son and said, "This way."

Zak opened the basement door, turned on the light, and watched as the two men stepped carefully down the stairs.

"It's over to the right," Ben Fisher said in a voice that faded away.

Zak went to the back door and turned off the deck light. He and Chloe listened to the night sounds. Then the door from the garage opened and closed, and soon afterward Mr. Dale walked into the kitchen.

"Is he here?" Mr. Dale asked, looking around.

"Yeah," Zak said. "He got here about five or ten minutes ago. The back way again."

"Good," Mr. Dale said, nodding.

"Oh, the son is here, too," Zak said. "Doug, I think his name is."

"I think we should turn off the lights," Mr. Dale said. "Maybe sit at the table. Try not to look suspicious."

28

1776, 1783, and 1789

"I believe someone in this class has gone above and beyond," Mr. Brown said.

The history students looked around, confused.

"The posters," he said, pointing to the two Lincoln posters that hung high on the wall behind Darius Brown's desk. "Who is responsible for our new wall decorations?"

Zak pointed at Mia Holmes, who sat across the classroom with her head lowered. Mr. Brown nodded at Zak and turned to Mia Holmes.

"Miss Holmes, thank you."

Mia looked up, surprised, then turned quickly and shot Zak a mean look.

"Excellent work. You have provided an inspiration for the class following our brief detour into the American Civil War." Mia turned back to look at the teacher and sat up straight. "Remember, as historians we must be vigilant, always asking ourselves what is important and what is trivia."

"Who's that picture of?" Candice Daniels said, pointing to the poster of Mary Todd Lincoln.

"Nobody," Zak shouted from behind Jeremiah Koll.

Darius Brown nodded and grinned at Zak.

"I'm going to start out with a question of my own," Darius Brown said. "Since you have been over this before, you will probably know the answer." He looked around. "When was George Washington elected president?"

"July 4, 1776," Fuzz Preston said quickly.

"Sorry."

"But that's the Fourth of July," Beth Sanders said.

"It is. It is also the wrong answer. Anybody else?"

"When the war was over."

"Ah. And when was the war over?"

"1777?"

Darius Brown shook his head.

"1778?"

"Keep going," Darius Brown said.

"Wasn't it 1783?" Betty Ng said uncertainly.

"Very good, Miss Ng. The war ended in 1783 with the Treaty of Paris," Darius Brown said. "So George Washington was elected president in what year?"

"1783?" Dez Mitchell asked tentatively.

"It was 1789, wasn't it?" Betty Ng said.

"It was, Miss Ng. 1789."

"Why did it take so long?" Nick Draves asked.

"That is precisely the question I want to ask you, Mr. Draves," Darius Brown said. Nick Draves looked around nervously. "There are only three dates you will need to remember in our study of the American Revolution. One is the year George Washington became the first president of the United States of America. Mr. Mould?"

"Betty just said it. Wasn't it 1789?" Moleman said.

"Correct," Darius Brown said. "The second is the year the American Revolutionary War ended. With the Treaty of Paris."

"Hey, you're going backwards. That's not fair," Nicole Anderson said.

"What was that year, Miss Anderson?"

"It was 1783," Nicole Anderson said. "But you're still going backwards."

"Correct," Darius Brown said. "And the third is 1776. Mr. Draves?"

"Um...Independence Day. I mean Independence *Year*," he said.

"Why is that important? Mr. Dale?"

Zak had gained confidence in his history class. He felt he could say almost anything and not be judged or feel bad, even if he gave the wrong answer. He also felt that if he thought about the people in history—the famous and not-so-famous—they would feel and act and think a lot like he did.

"That's the year when we declared our independence. When the people got together and said 'Enough is enough.' When people thought more about America than just themselves."

"It was also, as you so eloquently said in a previous class period, 'when people first started to think of themselves as Americans.' Do I have that right, Mr. Dale?"

Zak nodded once, his face red with embarrassment.

"Each of the thirteen colonies got fed up with Great Britain and what we call the Coercive Acts established by Parliament," Darius Brown continued. "The colonies got together—at the Second Continental Congress—shortly after fighting started with the battles of Lexington and Concord and said 'No' to all the rules and regulations and taxes established by the British Parliament, and then 'No' to the rule of King George the Third."

"But they were already fighting. So why did they need a piece of paper?" Jason Wiley asked.

"Good question," Darius Brown said. "Tell me, what was the Declaration of Independence? Mr. Koll?"

"It's that 'enough is enough' paper Z was talking about," Jeremiah Koll said.

Zak was struck by the fact that a star football player at school had listened to him and knew his name. It was a strange feeling. He'd lived his life trying to hide, trying not to attract attention, trying to be an unknown, and here he was being quoted by somebody. It felt good.

"Correct, Mr. Koll," Darius Brown said. "But it's more than just 'enough is enough,' although that's part of it. The Declaration of Independence is an announcement of America's right to be treated as an equal. Not owned by anybody else. Not ruled by anybody else. Independent as individuals and as a country. It is a declaration that we are Americans, not colonists. Listen to this: 'We hold these truths to be self-evident, that all men are created equal, that they are endowed by their Creator with certain unalienable Rights, that among these are Life, Liberty and the pursuit of Happiness.'"

"Isn't that just justifying what they'd already started?" Katie Ramerez asked.

"Explain your meaning, Miss Ramerez," Mr. Brown said.

"I mean...I mean," she stuttered, "the war was already going on, right?"

"That's right," Darius Brown said.

"So they just wanted to make it clear why they were all mad and everything," Katie Ramerez said. "And make up a lot of reasons why it was so important. So it would look good."

"Very insightful, Miss Ramerez," Darius Brown said. "So tell me…Miss Holmes…were they just words? Simple justification?"

"I think it's like in the law," Mia said. "Weren't a lot of these people lawyers?" Darius Brown nodded. "They wanted to make their case to the British and to the American people so it seemed all legal. Even though it wasn't."

"I don't get it," Bruce Fetzlof said. "What does she mean it wasn't legal? She makes it sound like they were a bunch of criminals."

"They were criminals, Mr. Fetzlof," Darius Brown said.

"I thought…they were…patriots," Trudy Taylor said, speaking as loudly as Zak had ever heard her.

"Actually, they were both," Darius Brown said. "Those who signed the Declaration of Independence and those who joined the military and fought against the British…they were all traitors. They risked everything."

"What do you mean 'they risked everything'?" Beth Sanders asked.

"These were not poor people. They were John Hancock, Samuel Adams, Benjamin Franklin, Thomas Jefferson, and lots of other important men. They were landowners. Professionals. People with money. If they lost, they lost everything—their jobs, their property, their savings, and their families—all for an idea. Oh…and their lives, too. Don't forget that. Traitors were put to death."

"I thought they were the good guys," Maggie Cho said.

"When you win you're called a patriot and get written up as a hero in the history books," Darius Brown said, holding up his history book. "When you lose, you're a traitor and they put a rope around your neck and hang you until you are dead."

"Oh," said Beth Sanders.

29

Sick Animals

Zak worried about his science presentation all during Band. He had stayed up until two in the morning finishing his speech. It was still rough, but not bad. He silently read it three times in English class. He could also work on it during Chemistry, but he had to be ready to deliver it in the science classroom after school. Fletcher said he would select the final speakers based on the results of the first round of presentations. Zak and Miles had signed up for the first group...the first of two. Only 15 students had volunteered, out of which five would be selected. He wasn't ready. He knew he'd never be ready.

"Quiet your instruments, please," Zak's Band teacher, Mr. Shapiro, said in a pouty voice. "I am a little depressed today. Yes, depressed. Do you want to know why I'm a little depressed today? Do you? It's because I had to listen to this band play at yesterday's game."

One of the reasons Zak stayed up so late the night before was that the freshman band had to play "The Star Spangled Banner" at the start of the girls' softball game. Zak played French horn, but not well, which was why he always sat in the last chair. Music wasn't one of his talents, and it didn't help that the keys on his French horn stuck so he couldn't hit the right notes. The mellophone he played at the games and marching band was even worse. Plus, he always seemed to lose his mouthpiece. At the game he had to borrow Kimberly Thompson's old mouthpiece, which almost made him sick. It had green things growing on it that he couldn't wipe off.

"Today we will begin work—again—on 'The Star Spangled Banner.' I realize that we learned this in our first month together, but after last night's so-called performance…well, as one critic told me, 'It sounded like a herd of sick animals.'" He paused. "Sick animals."

Zak knew this would be his last year in Band. He knew it and he didn't care. He never practiced and often pretended to play, hiding behind six-foot-tall Melanie Baskerville and the row of flutes in front of him. He also knew that others in the band—including several French horn players—did the same thing. They depended on Mitchell Fisher and Sari Narayanan to carry their section. They had talent and loved being in Band.

"Let me set the stage for our selection," Mr. Shapiro said. "It is the year 1814, near the end of the War of 1812. An unknown poet named Francis Scott Key watched as the British attacked the American troops at Fort McHenry during the night."

British? Again?

"In the morning, Key sees the American flag still standing above the fort and knows that the American troops survived. It is a song about bravery and patriotism and strength. It is inspirational. And it became our country's National Anthem in 1931."

Zak looked to his left, past Kimberly Thompson and David Hanson. There were two empty chairs he hadn't noticed before.

No Mitchell Fisher and no Sari Narayanan. He looked at Kimberly Thompson and, wide eyed, gestured with his battered French horn toward the two empty chairs. She swallowed hard.

"Our mission is to play this song perfectly in front of the entire graduating class and their families," Mr. Shapiro said. "That gives us only a couple of weeks, if my math is accurate."

Zak's only hope for this practice was that the sound of the French horns would be drowned out by the trumpets and the percussion section.

"Let me begin with the French horn section," Mr. Shapiro said.

Zak felt sick.

30

Pica Reactions

The science room looked remarkably clean and picked-up, even though weeks had passed since Zak had polished and cleaned everything. A few students came in late and sat in the back. An oppressive silence was broken only by the sound of Miles' strained breathing.

"Thank you for joining us today?" Dr. Fletcher said, standing and facing the audience. "Students, thank you for taking part in these preliminary presentations? I hope you will also join me in welcoming a few honored guests—judges who unfortunately cannot attend next Friday's presentation. Let me introduce Dr. Kenneth Watanabe and Dr. Lillian T. Rose. Dr. Watanabe is a professor of biological science at Wentworth College? Am I right?" Dr. Watanabe nodded. "Dr. Rose is a senior engineer for Alliance Systems? Correct?" Dr. Rose bobbed her head. "Please welcome our distinguished guests."

Scattered weak applause came from the twelve students in the room.

"Yes? Today we will hear presentations from several students.

The best of these will be selected to present at the first of our John Quincy Adams Science Series in the auditorium for the entire ninth grade class." He paused. "We will begin with Mr. Dale, am I right?"

Zak stood up and walked to the front of the classroom. He carried the four pages of his speech and two flimsy posters, which he set on an empty easel. He looked out at the audience and then at his paper. His hands shook like frightened animals.

"Whenever you are ready, Mr. Dale?" Dr. Fletcher said.

"Um, my report is called 'Neurobiology: The Amazing Brain,'" Zak began.

He looked around the room and saw Miles giving him a thumbs up, Kim Sather seemingly bored, and Betty Ng and Arlo Mould alert and possibly interested. Mia Holmes sat in the front row. Zak was happy to see her. He looked closer and saw that she was wearing a boy's maroon and white letter jacket. What was that all about? She gave him the peace sign.

"The human brain is an amazing machine," Zak read from his paper, not looking up. "It's about the size of a coconut, mostly made of water—about seventy-five percent—and weighs around three pounds."

As he continued, Zak managed to raise his head and make occasional eye contact with the judges in the back of the room—a university professor and an engineer. Why were they even here? Zak rubbed his eyes and focused on his speech.

"In Egypt, before someone was mummified, their brains would be removed through their nostrils. And some brains, like Albert Einstein's brain, were stored in jars like those for years."

Zak pointed to the jars on the shelf in the back of the classroom. Felix stared at him. Mia Holmes stifled a laugh.

"A doctor took out Einstein's brain after he died. And

147

Einstein's eyes were kept in a safe deposit box in New York City and then sold in 1994."

He heard the Moleman say, "Cool," after which Dr. Fletcher gave Arlo Mould a critical look from across the room.

"The cerebrum makes up the largest part of the human brain. About eighty-five percent. It's covered by these curly looking things which are nerve cells and called the cortex." He pointed to a fuzzy, pixelated photo of the brain on the easel. "There are one hundred billion nerve cells—called neurons—in the human brain."

Zak looked up. This was the part where he knew he could lose his audience, if he hadn't lost them already. He thought about skipping ahead but instead kept going.

"The cerebrum is separated into two parts: a right hemisphere and a left hemisphere. Or what's sometimes called a 'right brain' and a 'left brain.'"

He pointed to the sides of his own head.

"In the 1960s, a doctor named Roger Sperry operated on a person and removed part of her brain. The woman had been having seizures and Dr. Sperry thought he could help. After the surgery the patient seemed normal, except Dr. Sperry noticed that her personality seemed to be split into two halves, each half of which reacted to things in a different way. The left side did the verbal processing and the right side did the non-verbal processing."

Zak checked the time. He was fine.

"That research led to the discovery of left brain and right brain theory. Math and science and language on the left side of your brain and the more sensitive and imaginative side on the right. Most adults are left brain thinkers. They're more practical and organized and can do math and science pretty well. But many famous people like Shakespeare, Mozart, and Picasso were right brain thinkers. So were Einstein and Leonardo da Vinci, which is kind of surprising."

Dr. Fletcher was clearly enjoying the presentation.

"Even though most people are left brain thinkers, some studies have shown that most preschoolers start out as right brain thinkers. But because schools emphasize math, language, and logical thinking so much, at seven years old only about ten percent of kids are considered creative right brain thinkers, and only about two percent as adults."

Zak froze. He never really thought about that before, even when he was writing his speech. Different types of thinking, different types of intelligence. Not everybody's brain worked in the same way. Which meant that people could be smart in different ways. He shook his head, looked up, and cleared his throat. Felix's eyes locked on his. Dead armadillo stare. Somehow he found that encouraging and kept going.

"Brain studies have also been done of non-humans as well," Zak continued. "Elephant brains can weigh about 11 pounds, which is nearly four times as much as human brains. And some whales have brains that weigh as much as 20 pounds. With a bigger brain you might think they would be smarter than us. But they're not. So it's not the size of the brain that matters."

Zak looked at Miles.

"And animals can do things we normally associate with people. For example, elephants..."—Miles rolled his eyes—"... and chimps and dolphins can look in a mirror and recognize themselves. Baboons and chimpanzees can use language to express abstract ideas. An octopus can open jars. And cuttlefish have language and can communicate with people and even wink." Zak winked. "Even prairie dogs are pretty smart. There's a professor named Slobodchikoff, however you say it, who found that prairie

149

dogs can say things like 'tall human in yellow shirt,' 'short human in green shirt,' 'coyote,' 'deer,' and 'red-tailed hawk.' Except not in English like that. In prairie dog language."

Zak's mouth was dry but he was almost done.

"A lot more research needs to be done, especially on the relationship between the brain and teeth." Zak glanced at Dr. Fletcher, who almost jumped out of his chair. "Some scientists in Sweden have found that nerves in the brain connect directly to the nerves in the teeth." Dr. Fletcher wrote something on the paper in front of him. "When teeth are pulled out, people remember less and less." Dr. Fletcher was staring at him, smiling, looking at him with his big fish eyes. Zak wanted to end the speech as quickly as possible. "It's clear that the brain is an amazing organ. And that's something to think about. Thank you."

Zak exhaled slowly, blinked several times, and did a little bow.

Students and judges applauded politely, and Dr. Fletcher clapped vigorously and then jumped up and thanked Zak and introduced the next speaker, Kim Sather.

Zak sat down. He was exhausted. His armpits were soaked, so he tried to keep his elbows close to his body. He looked at Mia Holmes. She leaned over.

"That was great, Z," she said. "Really interesting. Especially the parts about the prairie dogs and Einstein's eyeballs."

"Thanks," Zak whispered back. "And thanks for coming."

Zak was so happy to be done that he pretty much ignored Kim Sather's presentation on single cell organisms, as well as the other presentations on chicken varieties, fiber optics, and endangered animals.

Miles came after that. He walked to the front of the science room holding an inch-thick stack of papers and a grocery bag. He set the report on the podium and unloaded bags of potato chips, corn chips, and other snacks onto the table next to him.

"Welcome. Thank you for coming," Miles began, making eye contact with the guests who sat at the back of the room. He seemed unusually nervous and firmly gripped the thick report. Several students nodded, one coughed.

"My complete research paper, which will be available after the presentation and also on my website, is titled, 'The First Snack: An Empirical Analysis of Sodium Chloride-based Snack Foods in Triggering Pica Reactions in *Homo sapiens*.' Or, as I like to call it, 'Bet You Can't Eat Just One.'"

Miles still sounded stuffed up, like he had a bad cold.

"As we all know, *Homo sapiens*—that is, people—require food to live. But the type of food we eat has changed through the centuries. Tens of thousands of years ago our ancestors lived mostly on meat, but they also ate plants, eggs, nuts, and roots."

Miles took a deep breath.

"Along with hunger for food, these shaggy bipeds had a craving for salt. Why? Because the body can't produce salt, and it's necessary for energy and for brains to function and for survival. Salt helps transmit electrical impulses so muscles can flex, hearts can beat, and brains can think."

Miles took another gulp of air.

"We need salt. In fact, our bodies crave salt. They always have. They crave it when we're hungry, thirsty, nervous, bored, or need minerals in our diet like iron. In other words, we crave salt pretty much all the time."

Laughter.

"This craving—what scientists call a pica reaction—is why we love hamburgers, hot dogs, pizza, and snack foods like chips, French fries, and cheese puffs. Salty foods help to satisfy these cravings."

151

Another deep breath. Miles' forehead glistened with sweat.

"Our love of and need for salty foods today begs the question: what were the potato chips of 10,000 B.C.?"

Miles turned the page in his notes. Another breath. He looked ready to faint.

"My answer to that question is the result of exhaustive research," Miles said. "I used microscopic analysis and simple mathematics to identify the composition of a wide range of salt-infused snacking products: potato chips, corn chips, pretzels, popcorn, cheese doodles, and pork rinds."

He stopped and took two deep breaths, then awkwardly spread out his right arm to indicate the bags of snack products he had set out on the table.

"My findings point to an indisputable correlation between these contemporary snacking products and a 'product,' I guess you could call it, as old as man—and woman—himself or herself."

Miles took a breath and then held up his left hand. His entire arm was shaking.

"I have that ancient product here with me today," he said.

Miles then rotated his hand so the knuckles and fingernails of his open hand faced his audience. He drew his fingers together into a fist and then, unexpectedly, stuck out the smallest finger of that left hand.

Miles looked around the science room, took a breath, exhaled, and jammed the finger into his left nostril. He held it there for two seconds and then lowered it slowly, slowly.

There was a collective gasp in the classroom.

Clinging to that single extended pinky fingertip was the Mother of All Mucus—the Babe Ruth of Boogers, the Sultan of Snot—nearly two inches tall and looking like a small greenish totem pole.

"Boogers. The original snack food," Miles announced loudly. Then all hell broke loose.

"Mr. Beakman," a voice began.

"When you examine the composition of common salty snacks…"

"Mr. Beakman." Dr. Fletcher's voice.

"About sixty percent carbohydrates…"

"Mr. Beakman." More agitated.

"About thirty percent fat…"

"Mr. Beakman." Dr. Fletcher stood up. His face was red.

"Seven percent protein and about one and a half percent salt…"

"Mr. Beakman." Dr. Fletcher growled.

"You'll find a statistically significant commonality with dry mucus. Boogers, if you will. Our oldest snack food."

"Mr. Beakman. That…will…be…enough!" Dr. Fletcher shouted, throwing down his notebook and stomping toward the front of the room.

Dr. Fletcher stood in front of Miles Beakman, blocking the speaker from the startled students and judges. He turned away from Miles, bowed slightly, and said to the audience, "On behalf of the faculty and staff of John Quincy Adams Senior High School, I apologize for this gross and distasteful display that Mr. Beakman has presented as science." Dr. Fletcher picked up Miles' presentation and began to tear it in half. "A childish prank." Fletcher struggled with the large document. "You can be sure that this irresponsible act will not go unpunished."

Dr. Fletcher looked around the room.

"Perhaps a slight break—five minutes or so—to clear the air, as it were, before our next presentations?" Dr. Fletcher added, still furious.

Miles remained in place with the salty booger standing erect on his little finger.

Zak was frozen. He didn't know what to say or do.

"I will recommend suspension, Mr. Beakman," Dr. Fletcher snarled in Miles' ear. "You have made me a laughingstock and irrevocably tarnished the image of this school." Dr. Fletcher stepped back a little. He looked ready to explode. Still staring at Miles he said, "Now go. Go. I will deal with you later."

31

Good Science

Miles leaned back against lockers 327 and 328 outside the science room and let out a sigh. Zak offered him a cinnamon candy. He shook his head, pulled out a Kleenex, and blew his nose hard.

"I can't believe you did that," Zak said.

"Blow my nose?" Miles said.

"You know what I mean," Zak said.

"I knew it was risky, but I had to do it," Miles said, blowing his nose again.

"Fletcher's going to kill you."

"That's his problem," Miles said. "All he sees is the boogers. He can't see the research. It's frustrating."

"You could've said 'mucus' or something like that."

"It's not a swear word," Miles said. "Besides, it was a presentation. You have to get people's attention. It's 'mucus' in my report. I just needed to jazz it up a little for this. Tweak Fletcher a little bit."

"You certainly did that," Zak said. "And picking your nose

155

was maybe a little over the top."

"What's crazy is that this is the first high school project I actually cared about," Miles said dejectedly. "I asked myself the question, 'Why are snack foods so popular?' and went from there."

"My opinion? I thought it was amazing, even though we only heard a minute of it," Zak said. "It made my brain speech look like second grade."

"No," Miles said. "You did good. You did what Fletcher wanted…what I probably should have done. It was great."

"It was just a speech," Zak said.

Miles and Zak stood for nearly a minute without saying anything. Miles took deep, satisfying breaths through his nose. Zak stood uncomfortably, moving his weight from his right to his left foot, not sure what to say. A short time later they heard footsteps coming down the hallway and around the corner. They looked at each other and then in the direction of the sound. It was coming closer.

"I thought everybody was gone," Zak said.

Miles nodded.

They waited, watching as Dr. Kenneth Watanabe turned the corner and walked toward them. He was about six feet tall with dark hair, glasses, and Japanese features. His dark gray suit, black shoes, red necktie, and white cotton shirt were immaculate. He stopped abruptly about a foot away from Miles.

"Excellent research, Mr. Beakman," Dr. Watanabe said. He held up the mangled, partially-torn copy of Miles' research paper that Dr. Fletcher had tried to destroy. "That's good science."

Dr. Watanabe turned and walked away, his perfectly shined shoes squeaking slightly on the floor.

32

Benkelman

Zak was alone in the house. He sat on the couch watching an animated movie from Japan called "My Neighbor Totoro." He was relaxed, happy the day was nearly over.

The phone rang. The name "Operator" came up on Caller ID and Zak picked up the phone.

"I have a collect call from a Mrs. Gloria Morris. Will you accept this call?" said a fuzzy voice.

"Um, sure. Yes," Zak said.

"Thank you. You may go through," the operator said, then disappeared.

"Hello?" Zak said.

"Zak? Is this Zak? This is your grandmother Morris."

"Grandma? Hi," Zak said. "Um...did you know you're missing?"

"I suppose so, but it certainly doesn't seem that way." She chuckled.

"Mom's worried."

"I'm perfectly fine," she said.

"Where have you been?"

"Where *haven't* we been! We were in Sioux City, Iowa. Stopped for some pie at a wonderful restaurant. We were in Omaha and Grand Island in Nebraska. Got a little rain, but it's mostly been dry. Dry as a bone. They could certainly use the rain. Now we're on our way to Denver."

"Colorado?"

"Yes, Colorado. I always wanted to see the mountains—and the Pacific Ocean, of course. All that blue water. Your grandfather never did like to travel. 'Everything we need is right here in Minnesota,' he used to say. He said that visiting other places gave a person 'ideas.' Meant you weren't happy with where you were. Couldn't change that man. Married for sixty-one years and I couldn't budge him a bit."

"I thought you used to live in New York."

"As a child, yes," she said. "A long time ago. I remember the World's Fair in 1939. Drove down in my father's old Ford. It was July. Steamy hot, but like a dream. Automobiles and televisions and the planetarium. The future! And all those people. Oh, New York was grand."

"Where are you now?"

He heard her voice from a distance. "Miriam, what is the name of this city? Benkelman?" Then the voice was back. "Zak? We're in Benkelman, Nebraska. Near the borders of Kansas and Colorado. Nice little town."

"What are you doing there?"

"Having the time of my life, if you want to know the truth," she said, laughing. "Back a ways, Miriam let me drive the convertible and"—her voice became hushed for a moment—"I got it up to 93 miles per hour." She laughed. "I know it's not legal. There are speed limits, and I don't think you should be doing it. And don't

158

tell your mother. But it was so liberating."

"Wow," Zak exclaimed. "Did you have the top down?"

"Oh, my dear! Lost my hat. It just flew away. And my hair. Oh, Zak, you should see my hair. I look a sight! These convertibles are just terrible for hair."

"Mom's real worried."

"Is Susan—your mother—there?"

"No," Zak said. "Everyone's gone. Except me."

"I'll call back. Just let everyone know that Miriam and I are fine. We're doing something I wish I'd done years ago."

"Grandma," Zak said. "I want you to know…"

"Yes, Zak? What's that?"

"Grandma," Zak said, his throat tightening up. "You're my hero."

33

Snot Man

The cafeteria was a mass of bodies and noise. Conversations, chewing, and antiseptic background music filled the room. Natural light came flooding in from skylights and formed patches of white light across the floor and tables and students. Zak sat at the loser table reading the book *Man Plus* by Frederik Pohl. Miles sat down next to him.

"What are you doing in this lunch?" Zak said, surprised. He slid a napkin between the pages of his book, closed it, and stuffed it into his backpack.

"I skipped out of biology and didn't have anything else to do so I thought I'd check out the food."

"Take a look," Zak said, gesturing with his plastic fork toward a lifeless, half-eaten burrito, orange-colored rice, soggy black beans, and some kind of mystery pudding. "Mexican surprise, they call it."

"Maybe I'll just skip lunch, too," Miles said listlessly, his eyes fixed on the tray of food.

"What's with skipping classes?"

Miles shrugged his shoulders. "What's the point?" he said.

"You should be flying high after what that judge told you about your research," Zak said.

"Fletcher tracked me down," Miles said. "Pulled me out of math to give me this." Miles removed a piece of paper from his backpack and tossed it next to Zak's lunch. Zak picked it up and read the handwritten note.

> *"Although your research appears to be sound and, I must admit, rather thorough, I am scandalized by your choice of subject matter. 'Boogers' is not a topic suitable for scientific research. It is a frivolous subject that is better suited to a kindergarten playground. It pokes fun at the entire scientific establishment and does not represent the level of seriousness I expect from the students at this high school. I see no merit in this research paper whatsoever. I have spoken with your science teacher, Mr. Moody, as well as the administration."*

"This is bogus," Zak said. "And Moody can't do anything to you. Neither can Petrovich or Decker." Zak forked some orange rice into his mouth, chewed, and swallowed. "Besides, it's all over school. You're like some kind of folk hero."

"Yeah, right," Miles said sarcastically. "'Snot Man.' I'm everybody's hero."

Miles looked across the table at Violet Granderson, who was rhythmically eating her food one thing at a time.

"I never saw it coming," Zak said. "That whole booger thing, I mean."

"I didn't blow my nose for an entire month," Miles said. "Do you know how hard that is?" He leaned toward Violet Granderson. "How's it going, Violet?" he asked.

Violet Granderson didn't look up. She didn't talk and barely seemed to breathe.

"You could have told me," Zak said.

"I didn't want to spoil the surprise," Miles said, looking back at Zak with a broad smile. "Besides, I wasn't sure I could pull it off."

"Like I said, it was classic," Zak said. "I didn't have a clue where you were going with all that about junk food and cravings and the Holy Grail."

Violet Granderson stood, grabbed her tray, and walked away from the table.

"I was planning on the left nostril for the first round and the right nostril for the big event," Miles said. "Right now—since I'm banned from any presentations—I finally have clear nasal passages."

"I just wish there was some way I could help," Zak said.

"It's not your problem," Miles said.

34

A Sign

Zak arrived at his science class ahead of time. As he entered the classroom, he again had a sense of satisfaction seeing all the clean surfaces and the orderly arrangement of the glassware, the Bunsen burners, and even the containers of kitty litter.

"Mr. Dale? Your presentation? I must commend you," Dr. Fletcher said, rising on his toes and then flattening his feet on the floor. "Well researched, presented clearly, and no..." He paused, trying to find the right word. "Surprises? Is that right?"

Zak nodded.

"Neurobiology is an exciting field, is it not? Your report could, perhaps, include a bit more depth. Flesh it out, as it were. Especially that fascinating information on teeth and memory. I was most intrigued. Yes?"

Zak nodded. He knew that if he was going to do well and beat Kim Sather, he needed to play to his audience. That was why he had included the part about teeth, even though Miles thought he was selling out.

Dr. Fletcher was talking to him again. He forced his brain to listen.

"A few more things, Mr. Dale?"

"Yes, Dr. Fletcher? Yes?"

The teacher stood with crossed arms, his head bouncing slightly. Zak noticed the vest. Dark blue. Corduroy. With gold buttons.

"Visual aids, Mr. Dale? Do you understand?"

"Visual aids?"

"Your presentation could do with a little more appeal, don't you think? Pizzazz?"

"You mean, like, pictures? Posters? That sort of thing?"

"Exactly. Exactly. Photographs. Models of the brain. Projections."

"I suppose I can do that."

"That will be fine, Mr. Dale," Dr. Fletcher said. "Our little event next Friday will include five presentations: yours, Miss Sather's, Mr. Crady's, Miss Vrek's, and Mr. Randall's speech on new frontiers in dentistry."

Zak nodded. Eric Randall's report was a slam dunk. Everybody knew it. Eric wasn't proud. When asked, he said he did it for the grade. And why not? Half the class thought about doing something on teeth or dentistry. Eric Randall was the only one who had gone through with it, and now he was in the top five.

"Thanks for picking me, Dr. Fletcher," Zak said. He thought about Miles' speech and quickly added, "I mean, I appreciate your confidence in me."

Like everything else, it was all a game. He never felt good about playing games like that. He also felt like a traitor to his best friend.

"Oh, Mr. Dale?" Dr. Fletcher said. "I have been meaning to mention your recent test."

"Test?"

"On the periodic table?"

"Yes?"

Zak steeled himself.

"Admirable."

"Really?" Zak said, surprised.

"You have made great strides this year, wouldn't you say?"

"Yes? I suppose. I have."

"There's a whole world of science out there, Mr. Dale. Good luck."

Zak nodded and turned to find his seat in class. As he did, he thought about his reason for taking part in the science presentations: money. He was hoping for that summer job, and now that he was in the top five and an "admirable" student, he felt an uncommon sense of accomplishment and confidence bubble up inside himself. He turned back to his teacher.

"Dr. Fletcher," he said. "Have you decided on the summer job?"

"Job?" The fish eyes stared at him. "Yes, a difficult choice, Mr. Dale." Fletcher's eyes turned to look up at the ceiling. "At this point I must say that I'm waiting for a sign."

35

Mist

The clouds were heavy, dark, and gray, and moved sluggishly across the sky. A fine mist hung in the air, enshrouding everyone and everything. It was as if the weather was confused and couldn't decide what to do. As he walked home, Zak looked toward the hidden sun, which was a faint glowing circle through the clouds.

"Hi, Z," Mia Holmes said, jogging up from behind him.

"Oh, hi," Zak said, surprised.

Mia was wearing the maroon and white letter jacket. It had a basketball and a football and several chevrons on the sleeves. She looked stiff and uncomfortable, and as she smiled Zak could almost see the unevenness of her teeth. Almost.

"I haven't…you haven't been around," Mia said.

"I've been busy," Zak said. "You know. Stuff. Like that."

"Congratulations on the science presentation," she said.

"Thanks," he said. "And thanks for being there."

They stood in silence and at the same time looked at the sun struggling to burn through the clouds. The mist stroked their faces like the touch of an angel.

"How's…Kevin?" Zak said.

"Kevin?"

"With the jacket," he said, nearly touching the fabric but holding back.

"Oh. He's okay," she said. "I didn't even remember I was wearing it."

"I see you in it all the time," Zak said. "I'm just saying," he added.

"You don't understand, Z," Mia said edgily. "You don't know what it's like with people always trying to hit on you and give you their number and 'Hey, baby' and all that."

"So that's why you wear it?"

"It's not that I like Kevin," she said. "In fact, he and his friends are pretty juvenile."

"Then…why even hang around with him?"

Mia closed her eyes hard, like she was holding back some kind of pain, and then opened them again.

"It keeps all those annoying people away and all the things they say," Mia said. "It's like…a shield."

"A shield? Like Captain America?" Zak asked.

"I was thinking more like the goddess Athena, actually."

They laughed.

"But hold it," Zak said. "You're talking to me."

"That's because you can see past the shield. You see me, the person. There's only a few who can do that."

"I have to admit that it kind of keeps me away," Zak said, nodding. "The jacket."

"Sorry," she said. "I didn't think about that."

"And Kevin?"

"He's got what he wants. A pretty girl to wear his jacket like he owns her," she said. "But I don't matter. I could be anybody."

"I never thought about that, either."

"It does get kind of complicated," she said.

"What about with other girls? Doesn't wearing the jacket make them mad?"

"Nah," she said. "It's like you're in some kind of club. You don't have to do anything or know anybody. You're in."

"And you're part of the group?" Zak asked.

"That's right," Mia said. "Of course, behind your back they all hate you."

"It is complicated."

"It's the same everywhere," Mia said.

"Can't you just give the jacket back?" Zak asked. "What could they do? What would happen?"

"They'd turn on me in a second. All of them. Especially the girls," Mia said. "Girls can be nasty. Worse than boys."

"Everybody can be mean," Zak said.

"This is different," Mia said. "If you're not in the group, you don't matter."

"Like me," Zak said.

"You, Miles, and most everybody else in school," she said.

"That's not a bad thing," Zak said. "I'm all about not mattering."

"There's…hatred there, too," she said quietly.

"What does that mean?" Zak asked uncertainly.

"I'm talking about Mr. Brown," Mia Holmes said.

She faced Zak and they looked at each other. Zak scrunched up his face.

"Because he's…because of his color?"

Mia slowly nodded.

"I didn't think that mattered," Zak said, flustered.

"It does to some people," Mia said. "More than you might

think."

Zak thought about things he'd heard about Mr. Brown—whispers in the hallways, the way some people talked, the drawing on the whiteboard, even the looks. It was all in a sort of code. He wasn't sure he wanted to hear what Mia was saying. He had always prided himself on staying apart, keeping his distance, not getting involved. Aside from his own family and a few friends, he was an island. Is that what independence was about? The freedom to be alone? Or did it mean to be part of something larger? He didn't know. He thought about Mr. Brown and what the teacher said in class about being independent and willing to fight for something. It was so much easier to do nothing.

"Is there anything we can do?" Zak said.

The mist had turned to rain, which began to fall in larger and larger drops. Mia lowered her head.

"I have to go," she said.

36

The Call

The phone rang.

"Can you get that, Zak?" Mrs. Dale said from a distance. She was in the kitchen cutting up vegetables for a stir fry.

Zak walked slowly to the phone and looked at Caller ID. Fisher Electric, it said. Zak picked up the phone.

"Hello?"

"Yeah," said a voice, "this is Doug Fisher. We worked on the electrical the other day."

"Do you want to talk to my dad?" Zak asked.

"I was just going to drop off the invoice for the work," he said.

Mr. Dale entered the room.

"Here's my dad," Zak said, handing the phone to his father.

"This is Bill Dale."

Pause.

"Yes, yes, of course. I remember."

Pause.

"Everything seems to be working. Thank you."

Pause.

"Maybe you can mail that. Or I'll pick it up. I can be over tomorrow morning."

Pause.

"You're where?"

Mr. Dale's head jerked up, his eyes flashed open, and he hurried to the living room, almost knocking over Zak. He looked out the window. In the driveway was a red van with the image of a large electrical plug and the words "Ben Fisher & Son Electric."

Bill Dale buried his head in his right hand.

37

The Adams Oak

English class, second hour.

Zak sat at his desk and looked out the window, trying not to think about anything. His English teacher, Mr. Larkin, was introducing a new unit on *Lord of the Flies*. Mr. Larkin was a large, almost obese man with yellowing skin and a full beard. As he moved around the classroom passing out worn paperback copies of the book, Zak noticed the long, dark, thick hairs that grew on the backs of the teacher's fingers.

"This is a book about what might happen if young men and women like yourselves ruled the world," Mr. Larkin said. "Kids are stranded on an island after the plane they're in is shot down."

"I heard this is boring," Levi Dweck said. He was a skinny, dark-featured boy with black curly hair and glasses. He thought everything was boring.

"It can be a challenging novel," Mr. Larkin said. "But if you open your mind to it, there's action, adventure, savagery, murder… everything you could hope for from a good movie or TV show."

"Can't we just watch the movie?" Vikki Plummer asked. She

was under five feet tall but had the longest hair in the school—nearly to her knees. According to Vikki, her hair had never been cut.

"Yes…for extra credit," Mr. Larkin said. You couldn't see his smile through the beard, but it was there. "Compare and contrast. Two pages."

Zak's mind wandered. He thought about Miles and Dr. Fletcher and the presentation. It didn't seem fair, but there was nothing he could do to make it right for his friend.

"Is this our last book?" Jeremiah Koll asked. Jeremiah sat on the opposite side of the room from Zak.

"Yes, this is our final unit of the year," Mr. Larkin said. "There are some good discussion topics here. We'll be able to break into small groups. And I have some survival games we can play."

Zak's chair was closest to the window. He could see the school entrance with the John Quincy Adams Senior High School sign and the massive oak tree. The Adams Oak. Right then, the branches stuck out like ancient black animals, and the new leaves fluttered like butterflies just out of their cocoons.

"Let's spend our class period reading the book," Mr. Larkin said. "If you can get through chapters one and two we'll have something to discuss tomorrow."

There was a collective sigh from the class and everyone started talking, texting…doing everything but reading. Only a few students actually looked at the book.

Zak opened the novel to the first page. Chapter One. "The Sound of the Shell," he read. "The boy with fair hair lowered himself down the last few feet of rock and began to pick his way toward the lagoon. Though he had taken off his school sweater…"

That was as far as Zak could manage at 8:30 in the morning. He preferred to read at night when he could pick the time and place and have some music playing in the background. He turned to face the window and pretended to read. Shell…rocks…lagoon… school sweater. Zak hated to read books for school. Even good books. He could never enjoy what he was reading. He always had to be thinking about character development, descriptive language, themes, epiphanies, and symbolism. Where was the fun in that?

Right then something caught his eye. He lowered the book and leaned closer to the window. There was something hanging from one of the large branches of the Adams Oak. It looked like a white rope. A white rope with a circle at one end. A…noose. He looked around the classroom. Mr. Larkin was busy at his desk and the rest of the class was just there. Nobody saw what Zak saw. He felt sick. Sick and ashamed. He knew he had to do something, but he wasn't allowed to leave class or leave school.

Zak couldn't concentrate for the rest of the period, and when the bell rang he was almost numb and still didn't know what to do. Go to the office? Talk to a teacher? Talk to the principal? He finally noticed Mr. Larkin staring at him.

"Is there something…?" Mr. Larkin began.

"No. Sorry. No. I've got to go," Zak said, and picked up his books and joined the flow of students moving through the hallways.

Without really thinking about it, Zak maneuvered his way through the groups and the slowpokes and the clumps of popular girls and the mass of moving flesh and made his way out through the main doors. Nobody stopped him. Nobody cared. They were all worried about themselves and getting to class. Zak tried to look casual as he walked down the sidewalk toward the parking lot. He glanced up at the sky. A few shapeless white clouds covered the blue. The sun seemed to direct all its rays at Zak as if to melt or transmute him. He kept walking until he was close to the big oak tree. He stared at the rope swaying in the light breeze. Who would do something like that? It was a symbol. A terrible symbol that sent a clear message: hate. Lynchings and murders of black people and horrible, cruel, animal things.

Suddenly Zak felt small. If he were tall, he might be able to jump and grab the noose and pull it down. But he didn't have a chance. The only way was to climb.

He looked around, set his books at the base of the tree, jumped up, and wrapped his arms around the trunk. It was enormous and the bark cut into his palms and forearms. He had about five feet of climbing to get to the lowest branch. Zak hugged the tree with his legs, wrapped his arms higher on the trunk and then pulled his lower body up. It was hard work, but he gradually made his way up the oak tree until he could grab hold of the lowest branch. After that he was able to scurry up the last few feet. Then he sat on the large arm of the tree breathing hard. Zak looked around. Nobody else seemed aware that he was up there. It was as if he were truly invisible.

He looked ahead and saw the white rope wrapped around the tree limb about 10 feet away. Zak shinnied his way out to where the rope hung. It had been coiled around the wood three or four times, but not tied. The branch was about 12 inches in diameter, so Zak had to stay low and hold on so he didn't tip sideways. After a few seconds of awkward twisting and grabbing, he was able to unwind and gather up the rope. He held it in his left hand, smiling, satisfied that he'd managed to do away with some of the hate in the world.

As Zak silently celebrated his success, disaster struck. His body shifted, he lost his balance, tipped to his left, and fell. He had a sense of rotating in the air in slow motion and watching as the grass seemed to come at his face. He gritted his teeth, held the

175

rope tightly, and felt all his internal organs vibrate as he slammed into the ground.

He also heard a snap.

Zak lay motionless on the ground, face down. He felt a pain in his left arm, which was bent awkwardly under his chest. Even worse, he couldn't breathe. He stretched his mouth open as far as it would go, hungry for air, trying to make his lungs work. As his mind struggled to deal with the pain in his arm and the lack of oxygen, he heard a voice above him. It was loud and insistent and familiar. All he wanted to do was breathe, but the words managed to make their way through his mental fog.

A girl's voice.

"I don't know what you were doing up in that tree, and I really don't care. All can say is that I knew something like this was going to happen. I warned you. I'm the only one who was willing to tell you that you're out of your league. And was I right? Of course I was right."

Aurora. It was Aurora.

"I give you simple instructions," she continued. "'Be your normal, ordinary, boring self,' I said. How difficult is that? But you go and ignore everything I say and go hanging around that blondie and now, you're falling out of trees. Do you hear me? Am I getting through to you?"

Zak managed a feeble breath and tried to speak.

"Aurora," he grunted inaudibly.

"I'm sick and tired of being your babysitter. I already called 911, and I'm waiting until they arrive. I have better things to do with my time, you know. I'm on my way to class—which I'm missing right now without a good excuse or a hall pass, I'll have you know. Well, you certainly wrecked my day. Does that make you feel any better?"

Zak licked his dry lips and coughed. He sucked in a little more air.

"Oh, so now you're ready to talk. Well, I have half a mind to just turn around and leave right now."

"Aurora, please," he managed.

"'Please' won't get you anywhere with me, Buster Brown."

"Closer."

"What?" Aurora lowered herself to her knees and bent her head to listen to Zak. "Well? Are you ready to say, 'Aurora, you were right'?"

Zak leaned painfully onto his left side and dug his right hand underneath his body. His fingers closed tightly around the rope and pulled it out.

"Here," Zak said, pushing the rope into Aurora's hands.

"What? What's this?" she said, surprised. "Is this what I think it is?" She stood up quickly. "Oh, my God, Z. You are going to hell. That's it. You are literally going to hell. I'm washing my hands of you right here and now. This could get you expelled. You could be arrested!"

"No. I'll explain. Later."

"Sure. When it's convenient, you want me to cover up your little messes. Now you want me to be an accessory."

"Please. Just take it. Hide it."

"You owe me, Zak Dale," Aurora said fiercely, gritting her teeth. "You owe me big time."

Aurora looked around furtively and stuffed the rope into her giant purse.

Zak bent his head slightly to the side and saw Assistant Principal Petrovich and a school security guard—Archie something—headed toward him. A crowd of students stood just outside the school's front entrance. Zak tried to get up but decided against it.

"What's going on here," a man's voice said.

"Ask him," Aurora said. "I had nothing to do with it."

"Son, can you talk? Are you all right?" The man's voice was close.

He heard the sound of an ambulance in the distance.

"Just…lost…a…contact," Zak said weakly, and then passed out.

38

After the Fall

Zak and his family entered their house through the garage. Larry was waiting for them, his tail wagging excitedly.

"Can I get that hangy thing when you're done?" Chloe asked Zak, tugging at the sling around his neck.

"Chloe, be careful. He has to be careful of that arm."

"Sure. Yeah. You can have it," Zak said, pulling the strap over his head and handing it to his sister.

"Zak, the doctor said…," Mr. Dale said.

"He said not to get the cast wet. He didn't say I had to use that stupid sling."

"It's not stupid," Chloe said.

"Whatever," Zak said. "It's yours."

Chloe pulled the sling over her neck and trotted off in the direction of her bedroom.

"The doctor said it could have been worse," Mrs. Dale said, concerned. "It was just those two bones."

"Ulna and radius," Zak said.

"What I still don't understand is why you were up in that

tree," Mr. Dale said.

"I didn't do it, if that's what you mean."

"Of course not, Zak," Mrs. Dale said. "We know you wouldn't."

"Principal Decker and Assistant Principal Petrovich made it very clear that this is serious business," Mr. Dale said sternly.

"I know," Zak said. "Like I told them, I climbed up the tree and got the rope and fell and handed it to Aurora. I thought she'd be on my side."

"She did the right thing," Mrs. Dale said. "It's something for the school and the police to deal with."

"Zak, you can't just take that rope down and pretend it never happened," Mr. Dale said. "Hate crimes are serious."

"You have to get others involved," Mrs. Dale said. "To show that people who hate are the minority."

Zak nodded.

"It's not your battle," Mr. Dale said.

"It's the school administration's job," Mrs. Dale said. "It's a job for adults."

"Then where were they?"

"They can't be everywhere," Mr. Dale said. "Sometimes you have to be their eyes and ears."

"You should have talked to the principal," Mrs. Dale said.

"I didn't think about that," Zak said. "I just thought about getting the noose down before anyone could see it."

"Things need to be done in a certain way. There are rules and procedures that have to be followed," Mr. Dale said.

"So what happens now?" Zak asked quietly, resignedly.

"I think the police are through with you," Mrs. Dale said. "That's what the officer said."

"Mr. Petrovich said he thinks it was meant as a message to

some teacher," Mr. Dale said.

"Mr. Brown. My history teacher."

"I didn't even know you had another teacher," Mrs. Dale said.

"I told you Ms. Jackson was gone."

"But you didn't say anything about him being..."

"I didn't think it was a big deal," Zak said.

"What do you know about him?"

"Mr. Brown? He normally teaches at South High, but he's on some kind of special assignment at our school," Zak said. "He's great. Better than Ms. Jackson. We've been learning a lot about the American Revolution."

"Well, at this point you just need to back away," Mrs. Dale said.

"I'm not sure I can," Zak said.

39

Null

Night. Darkness.

Zak woke again to the call of the 2:19 freight train. He stared at the ceiling, feeling as though he had been awake for hours, and then he closed his eyes and listened to the shrill, sad cry, and involuntarily shivered. Years ago he'd put a penny on the railroad track and waited and then watched as a train passed by: barn-red cars with white graffiti, rusting green cars with closed sliding doors, black tank cars carrying unknown liquids, flat bed cars loaded with building materials. It was hypnotic, like watching the waves of the ocean. Later he found the penny flattened, Abraham Lincoln's face erased. He still had it in a drawer somewhere.

The train cut through prairies and mountains and fields and cities like a living animal, but without thought or feeling.

At his grandfather's funeral the minister had said, "'Ashes to ashes, dust to dust.'" That wasn't just people; it was everything. We're all of us moving toward death, Zak thought, and the sun and the stars and all the unknown worlds will some day grow cold and die. What does any of this matter? People, societies, worlds.

It had a purpose, maybe…but only for a moment in time. That moment could be to create something or to deface and destroy it. What was his life compared to everything else? He didn't matter. The universe knew that, if it had any kind of consciousness. He was nothing. Null. Zero.

Zak felt his arm begin to itch underneath the cast. He got out of bed and looked out the window. It was a clear night with an almost-full moon and bright stars. Zak looked for Mia's tattoo—Cassiopeia—but he didn't recognize anything except the Big Dipper, the three stars in Orion's belt, and the black emptiness that was bigger than everything. Perhaps Cassiopeia was no longer in the heavens, he thought. Maybe the stars had gone out.

Zak got back into his bed and fell asleep.

40

Defender of Justice

Zak spent his free period in the library with Miles. Mrs. Kaufman glared at them from her desk the entire time, as if concerned that Zak would desecrate some of her books, shelving, or computers. Zak had placed his arm with the cast silently onto the table and smiled at the librarian. She continued to stare. The cast was still foreign to him: big, clumsy, and purple. It fit through the arm holes of his Flash T-shirt with the lightning bolt on the front. The cast had just three signatures on it. Chloe had written her name in red marker but it looked like a large insect with big feet. Miles signed his name and wrote, "Break a leg." Mia signed her name in curvy cursive letters and underneath her name in big, bold capital letters wrote, "Z—DEFENDER OF JUSTICE!" Zak looked at the messages and smiled.

"I still can't believe Aurora turned you in," Miles said quietly.

"I know. It doesn't make sense," Zak said, flexing his fingers in the cast.

"She must have known you didn't do it."

"I suppose."

"I bet Petrovich…"

"He must've got hold of her."

"Once she got talking she probably couldn't stop," Miles said. "That's nothing new."

"Still, I asked her to hide it. I remember that."

"Any idea who did it?" Miles asked.

Zak shook his head. Mrs. Kaufman was still staring at him. He wondered if maybe he should ask her to sign his cast. Get on her good side. Nah. Wouldn't make a difference.

"I don't think the police will find anything," Miles said.

As the bell rang, Zak and Miles looked at the clock and gathered their books and notebooks. Zak managed to load up his backpack and sling it over his right shoulder with his good hand.

"Later," Miles said.

"Yeah," Zak said, still thinking about the incident.

Zak walked past Mrs. Kaufman, wiggling the fingers of his broken arm at her, then turned in the direction of his locker. The hallway was filled with bodies moving fast in both directions. He didn't notice the noise or the people. He kept his head down, found his locker, opened the metal door, and took out his lunch. Probably tuna again. He pulled an apple out of the bag and took a big bite. Gala. His favorite.

The cafeteria was down the hall to the right and then to the left. As he walked and chewed, a tall, red-headed, freckled boy wearing a letter jacket drifted from one side of the hall to the other in his direction. The boy kept coming and suddenly swerved and knocked him against the wall. Zak's backpack fell to the floor and the apple left his hand and rolled down the hall toward the bathrooms.

"Watch where you're going," the boy said, laughing. He was joined by another, taller boy he'd seen before. Kevin Rourke.

185

"What?" Zak sputtered, confused.

He knelt down and picked up his things with his one good hand, looking at the two who walked away laughing. The apple with one bite taken out sat in front of the water fountain. He left it.

Zak knew he'd been hit on purpose. But why?

Zak made his way to the cafeteria. As he crossed the floor and wove in and out between students with trays of hot lunch, he passed by the table with the football and basketball players. A foot suddenly stretched out in front of Zak and sent him sprawling onto the floor. The cast came down with a crack and his backpack slammed down beside him.

"Walk much?" said a voice from behind, followed by laughter.

Zak looked at the crowd at the table. They looked back, smiling, laughing, talking. He turned and sat down at the loser table, took out his lunch, smiled at Violet Granderson, and bit into the tuna sandwich. Zak wasn't invisible any more, and that made him nervous.

41

Reflection

The storm was a concert of violence. The rain fell in large, angry drops, striking every surface with a reckless fury. Lightning shot across the sky in a rage of white light, tearing up the dark sky. Massive thunderclouds paused overhead as if deep in thought, preparing for war. Water clawed and rushed out of the drain spouts and ran into the streets and gutters and storm sewers like a frightened creature returning to the earth.

"Maybe he didn't see it. It wasn't there for long," Mrs. Dale said, stabbing a piece of green pepper with her fork.

A thunderclap shook the house, rattling the cabinets, windows, and dishes. Larry yipped and ran into the laundry room to hide.

"Maybe," Mr. Dale said. "But you can't miss that van. It's bright red."

"Does it really matter?" Zak asked. "I mean, what can he do? It's not like he's a serial killer or anything."

"We don't know that," Mr. Dale said casually.

"Bill, let's not get anyone frightened," Mrs. Dale said quickly. "Mark has always been nice."

"You're right," Mr. Dale said. "There's nothing bad about using another electrician. It's like breaking up with someone. You just don't want them to feel bad."

"So is it better not to say anything…or to talk to him?" Mrs. Dale asked.

"I think you should talk to him," Zak said. "Isn't that what you tell us to do?"

A severe thunderstorm warning siren howled in the distance. Rainwater spilled out over the gutters.

"I look out there and all I can think of is Mother," Mrs. Dale said. "I hope she's safe."

"I'm sure she's fine," Mr. Dale said, chewing his food while looking out the window at the wall of rainwater. "She's a tough old bird."

"I should have talked to her…before," Mrs. Dale said. "She must have been so unhappy."

"Are you talking about Grandma Morris?" Chloe asked, moving white rice, carrots, peppers, and pieces of pork counterclockwise around her plate.

"You've been a good daughter, Susan," Mr. Dale said.

"I put her in that place. She obviously wasn't happy."

"It's not like she left for good," Zak said. "I mean, she's on vacation. She's having fun."

"Is she still escaped?" Chloe asked.

"Yep, still on the run," Zak said.

"Zak," Mr. Dale said.

"What? Be happy for her," Zak said. "I wish I was with her. It's not like you did anything bad. She's just feeling free. Maybe for the first time."

The lights flickered and went out.

"I thought the 'lectricity was fixed," Chloe said.

"This isn't just us. It's the neighborhood," Mrs. Dale said. "A tree might have fallen on a power line. I'm sure all the other houses don't have power, either."

Zak got up from the table and looked out the living room window.

"Dad?" Zak said. "You might want to take a look at this."

The rest of the family got up from the table and joined Zak at the picture window in the living room.

"Oh, my," Mrs. Dale said.

"What is it?" Chloe asked.

Every light in the neighborhood was off. Still, even in the graphite darkness and the pouring rain they could see a man standing in the middle of the street, naked except for white boxer shorts with red hearts. He stood staring at the Dale home with his arms drooping at his sides. His hair was pasted to his forehead. Water ran down his body and puddled around his feet. A flash of lightning cut through the sky and showed a ghostly white reflection on the streaming asphalt street. A boom of thunder shook the walls two seconds later.

"Mark," Mr. Dale whispered to himself.

"What's wrong with him, Daddy?" Chloe asked.

Zak felt the small hairs on his arms and the back of his neck stand on end.

"He's…sad, I think," Mr. Dale said.

"And wet," Zak added.

"You should do something, Bill," Mrs. Dale said.

"He could get lightninged," Chloe said.

Mr. Dale picked up a newspaper on a side chair and opened the front door. The sound of the storm and the pounding rain and the fresh cleansing smell now consumed the house. Mr. Dale stepped onto the walk, covering his head with the paper. The red maple in the front lawn swayed rhythmically in the wind like some enthralled worshiper at a revival meeting. Mr. Dale walked onto the driveway, the paper soaked and sagging on his head, and his feet sloshing among the puddles and streaming water. Butterscotch-colored worms, some more than ten inches long, lay squirming on the driveway.

"Mark!" Mr. Dale shouted through the tortured wind. "Mark! Come inside! Come inside!"

Mark Snyder stood still and seemed to stare at Bill Dale as if trying to identify who or what he was, then he turned and walked slowly, somnambulistically, back to his own house. Mr. Dale watched, the water soaking through his clothes. He waited until Mark Jenkins was inside his own house before walking slowly back up the driveway, along the walk, and to the door. Mrs. Dale, Zak, and Chloe looked at him from the inside, dry, with concerned faces.

"I think he saw the van," Mr. Dale said.

42

No Time

Zak waited for Mia Holmes near the doors at the school entrance. It had been days since he'd talked to her. He had waved to her in the hallways and in class and after school, but she was always with Kevin Rourke and his friends and a lot of other juniors and seniors. Zak didn't know how to deal with Mia's popularity. It made him uncomfortable. So he waited and hoped things would go back to the way they were before. It was like she'd been taken away. He looked at his cast and the words Mia had written: Defender of Justice. What did that mean? He knew it was a compliment, but he'd read and re-read it so many times he began to wonder if maybe she had been making fun of him.

Mia appeared down the hall talking with two senior girls. Girls he didn't know. Girls he didn't want to know. Mia looked over. Her eyes opened wide and a big smile appeared on her face.

"Z!" Mia shouted, rushing over to him. "How's your arm?"

Zak's face turned red as he saw students and teachers turn their heads to see where the commotion was coming from.

"It's fine," Zak said quietly, his head darting left and right in

191

embarrassment. "The doctor says everything's healing."

Mia reached out and touched the cast.

"I feel bad I haven't seen you," she said earnestly, racing through the words. "Things are just crazy. Some days I don't know what I'm doing or where I'm going. There's just no time."

"Mia! Are you coming?" one of the girls shouted impatiently.

Mia held up an index finger as if to pause everybody and everything except for the conversation with Zak.

"See what I mean?" Mia said exasperatedly.

"It's all right," Zak said.

"No. It's not," she said. "We're friends and you have that big presentation coming up and you need to win it."

"Win?" Zak said. "I'm hoping not to puke all over the stage."

"Mia! We don't have much time," a gum-chewing girl said, blowing a bubble.

"I need to slow things down," Mia said, looking away and then back at Zak.

"I guess I could use some help," Zak said. "With the speech, I mean."

"Call me," Mia said. "I mean it."

Mia looked toward her friends and started to move away from Zak.

"Sure," Zak said.

Zak watched Mia and her friends walk away talking and laughing. He thought he saw Mia look back, but he wasn't sure.

43

The Gran Cannon

"Dinner!" Mr. Dale shouted as he placed bowls of spaghetti noodles and sauce on the table, which joined a fruit salad of apples and oranges, four glasses of milk, and a cut up red pepper. Several "Just a minutes!" followed, and within five minutes all four Dales were seated at the dinner table. Larry positioned himself watchfully next to Chloe, who was the most likely to spill.

"Spaghetti! That's great," Zak said, grabbing the serving bowl and putting a mountain of noodles on his plate. He set that down, added the sauce, and then shook Parmesan cheese on top.

"How come we always have to eat like this?" Chloe asked.

"Like what?"

"With all of everybody," she said.

"We like to eat as a family," Mr. Dale said. "So we can check up on you and talk about the day."

"I heard from Grandma Morris today," Mrs. Dale said abruptly. "She's at the Grand Canyon."

"Cool," Zak said. "Then she got to see the mountains. That's what she wanted."

"What is that place?" Chloe asked.

"It's a famous National Park," Mr. Dale said. "The Grand Canyon is kind of a big hole in the ground. Very, very big."

"What did she say?" Zak asked his mother.

"She said she's fine. A little sunburned. Tired and sore. But she's doing fine. Both she and Mrs. Ramsey," Mrs. Dale said. "I guess they went…whitewater rafting."

"Grandma?" Zak said, laughing. "Rafting?"

"What's that? What's that?" Chloe asked, looking from face to face. Larry started barking in the excitement.

"Larry!" Mr. Dale shouted. The dog stopped barking but ran to the window to look outside.

"She said they were out rafting and camping for three days," Mrs. Dale said. "She said Miriam Ramsey almost fell in."

"Fell in what? The big hole?" Chloe asked.

"You're in a small inflatable boat on a river that moves very fast," Mr. Dale said. "It's called whitewater rafting."

"Now she's going to ride a mule down into the canyon," Mrs. Dale said. She shook her head. "I don't know what's gotten into her."

"We need to take a trip like that," Zak said.

Zak looked down at the end of the table and saw his mother crying, wiping her eyes on her napkin.

"What's wrong?" Zak asked. "Grandma's okay, isn't she?"

"Your mother is worried," Mr. Dale said.

Mrs. Dale tried to choke back the tears.

"Is that Gran Cannon a scary place?" Chloe asked.

"I want her to have fun, Zak. I do," Mrs. Dale said through her sobbing.

"What could be better? The Grand Canyon. The Rocky Mountains. A red convertible. A whitewater rafting trip. Riding a mule. I wish I was there with her."

"Grandma Morris may be trying to do too much," Mr. Dale said.

"She's having fun," Zak said. "I mean, she was at Golden Meadows basically waiting to die."

"That's not fair," Mr. Dale said. "She was happy there."

"Okay, maybe not to die. But to just kind of be there. What kind of life is that?"

"She had a good life, Zak," Mrs. Dale said.

"It's not over. You keep talking like it's over. There's lots of things she can do, and she's proved it."

"Did she say when she's coming home?" Mr. Dale asked his wife.

Mrs. Dale shook her head.

"I guess all we can do is wait," Mr. Dale said.

"I can't wait to find out where she goes next," Zak said.

44

Light

At the sound of the bell signaling the end of the first period, Mr. Brown shouted, "Read the rest of chapter six in your textbook for tomorrow, please," as the class rushed to get out the door. Zak was stuck behind Jeremiah Koll. Jeremiah always seemed taller to Zak every time he stood next to him. Over six feet tall and nearly 300 pounds.

"Man, this is a great class," Jeremiah Koll said to Zak.

Zak was surprised. Jeremiah Koll didn't talk much, and certainly not to him.

"Yeah," Zak said, watching Mia vanish through the doorway. "I never thought history could be like this."

"It's almost like it's right here, like we're living it," Jeremiah said. "Mr. Brown has to be the best teacher."

"Better than Ms. Jackson, that's for sure," Zak said.

"She would pee in her pants if she saw how he was teaching this class. Throwing out her tests and making fun of her questions," Jeremiah said.

Zak was just about to enter the noisy hallway when he heard

his name.

"May I speak with you, Mr. Dale?" Mr. Brown said.

"Sure. Yeah," Zak said uncertainly.

Darius Brown placed his hand gently in the small of Zak's back and led him outside the classroom door. Students streamed past in a noisy, turbulent flow. Mr. Brown turned to Zak.

"How is your arm?" he began.

"I didn't do it, Mr. Brown. Really," Zak sputtered.

Darius Brown held up his left hand to quiet Zak.

"I know that," Mr. Brown said. "Principal Decker and Assistant Principal Petrovich talked to me about what happened. Naturally, they did ask about you."

Zak didn't know what to say.

"Hanging a rope in front of the school while classes are in session is not the act of an intelligent human being. Would you agree?"

"Yes," Zak said slowly.

"You are far too intelligent to do something that foolish, Mr. Dale."

"Thanks...thanks for believing in me," Zak said.

"You did what you had to do," he said. He paused and reflected. "Probably what I would have done myself."

"Really?" Zak said, surprised.

"It is a natural reaction." The teacher clasped his hands together. "When you see something that offends you, you want to erase it like it was never there."

Zak nodded vigorously.

"That's what it was," Zak said. "I...I was really...ashamed... and I had to do something."

"At the cost of an arm."

"That's okay."

"It took a great deal of courage."

"I didn't really think about it," Zak said. "I was just looking out the window at the tree during English class."

Zak gestured in the direction of the tree and saw that his right index finger pointed directly at Kevin Rourke, who was walking on the other side of the hallway. Kevin looked Zak in the eyes. Zak gulped and turned back to look at his teacher.

"Studies have been done on something as simple as graffiti," Mr. Brown said. "Where it exists—where it is allowed to exist— it promotes other crimes and people feel less safe. Painting over graffiti, picking up litter, adding streetlamps instead of darkness… all these things matter. They show that people care."

"So are you saying that hiding the rope or covering it up was the right thing?"

"I don't think so," he said thoughtfully. "Hatred feeds upon itself. It shows its face in numberless places. It is best to shine a light on hatred. Show it for what it is…a terrible disease."

Zak shook his head. "I'm sorry," he said. "Most people are nice here."

"I have found that to be true," Mr. Brown said. "Of course, some would prefer that I return to South High School as soon as possible."

"Really?" Zak said. "You're the best teacher I've ever had. Jerry Koll was saying the same thing just a minute ago."

"Thank you for that, Mr. Dale," Darius Brown said.

"You're helping us understand history," Zak said.

"I am trying," the teacher said. "But I'm running out of time."

45

Astronomers

It was 9:37 in the evening. Zak was on the living room couch eating potato chips, flipping through his algebra textbook, and watching TV.

"Zak. The dog needs to go out," Mrs. Dale said.

"I've got homework. Have Chloe do it."

"Your sister's taking a bath."

"Can't she do it when she gets out?"

"Now."

"But..."

"You'll have more of a mess if you don't take the dog out now," she said.

"Okay, okay."

Zak slipped into some shoes, hooked the leash to the eager dachshund's collar, and opened the door. It was a cool evening and the sky was clear and black, revealing the light of hundreds of stars and a partial moon. Zak let the dog lead him along as he searched the sky. Larry wandered around the front yard, stopping to smell the grass every few seconds, occasionally looking up and

199

sniffing.

"Come on, Larry. Do your stuff," Zak said impatiently.

As he said this, a car came down the street and pulled into their driveway. It was Zak's father. The garage door opened and the car disappeared inside. A few seconds later the car door slammed.

Larry was preoccupied in the front yard and hardly noticed Mr. Dale in a dark suit and carrying a briefcase approach them.

"Hey, kid, how was your day?" Mr. Dale said, touching Zak's right shoulder.

"Fine."

Mr. Dale nodded and blew into his fist to keep it warm.

"Look, can you take care of Larry? I've got some homework to do," Zak said.

Mr. Dale smiled. "Tell you what," he said. "I'll stand out here with you for a bit."

They followed Larry around in the grass, glancing up at the night sky.

"Ever notice how, at night, dogs sniff and look for squirrels and rabbits, while people look up at the stars?" Mr. Dale said, breaking the silence.

"I guess I never thought about it."

"I think the first astronomers were shepherds and people like us walking their dogs. They looked up and started wondering about things."

They both raised their heads and listened to the sounds of their breaths and Larry's sniffing.

"Dad...I have a question."

"Okay."

"Miles did this science project—and it was really good—and Dr. Fletcher tore it up in front of the class. He said it was gross and disgusting."

"Was it?"

"Well…it was on snot. So that part may have been gross. But he did real scientific research and it was about 50 pages long. Lots better than mine."

"So what's the problem?"

"Dr. Fletcher picked me to give my speech in front of the whole class. I'm one of five." Zak paused. He found it hard to express what he was thinking. "I know I should be happy, but it doesn't feel right. I mean, how can I go up and give my presentation after what he did to Miles? He's my best friend."

"Is your speech any good?"

"It's okay. It's on the brain. But it's nothing like what Miles did. That was real science."

There was a pause.

Zak added, "I don't feel good about this. I don't want to let my friend down. It wasn't fair. But I can't change what's already happened. And if I don't give my speech, I'll probably lose my chance at that summer job and get a bad grade."

Mr. Dale continued to look up at the stars and shifted his briefcase from one hand to the other. In the distance, crickets and frogs made their own night music. There was a steady rhythm to it that seemed to pulse like the heart of some large organism. Together, they were part of that, father and son, alone together.

Mr. Dale turned to face Zak, the whites of his eyes almost glowing in the moonlight.

"Zak, there are times in your life when the choices you make are huge. If you're a soldier, say, or responsible for the jobs of hundreds of people. Or even when you have a family to support." He stopped, loosened his necktie, and let out a deep breath. Then he smiled. "This is not one of those times."

Mr. Dale let out a short laugh that surprised Zak.

"School is about learning. It's not about grades," Mr. Dale continued. "We sometimes forget that. All of us. Teachers and parents and kids. If it's something that matters, find a way to make it right. As long as nobody gets hurt."

"So my grade…"

Mr. Dale shook his head. "It doesn't matter."

"What other people think about me…"

Mr. Dale shook his head. "It doesn't matter."

Zak needed time to consider this. He was being given permission to do…something.

"I always thought you wanted me to get good grades and not get into trouble."

"I do. This doesn't change any of that."

"I don't get it."

"It's what you think of yourself," Mr. Dale said. "Do what's in your heart, son. You might be surprised what you learn."

Mr. Dale turned and headed into the house, leaving Zak and Larry in the darkness.

Zak looked up at the black sky dotted with faraway suns. Larry tugged at his leash ready to go back inside, but Zak wasn't ready. Not yet. Lost in thought, he found himself drawing imaginary lines among the stars.

46

The Fight

"Thanks for agreeing to help with the posters for my speech," Zak said. "You're a lifesaver."

Zak and Mia Holmes walked slowly toward Mia's house. The temperature was cool and the wind blew fiercely, which made Mia's blonde hair flutter like bird wings. She pushed the hair out of her face and pulled the letter jacket close around her. Zak looked down at the sidewalk and then at Mia. His oversized black hooded sweatshirt made him look like a walking shadow in the gray, overcast light. He didn't mind the cold. In fact, he found it refreshing. It kept him from thinking about speaking in front of the entire freshman class.

"Do you think you'll need some help during your speech?" Mia asked, searching for Zak's hidden, hooded eyes.

"For real?" Zak asked. He looked at Mia. He was surprised that she really seemed to care about him.

"Hey, if I'm helping with the poster, I need to make sure you don't mess up."

Zak laughed. "Actually...I'd really like that." He lifted his broken arm, which was a large bulge underneath the sweatshirt. "Fletcher wants me to have more visual aids, but it'll be impossible for me to talk and flip posters and hold up brains and things with my bad arm."

"You won't get disqualified if I'm up there with you?" Mia asked.

Zak shook his head.

"I don't think so. I'll ask Fletcher and maybe he'll take pity on me," Zak said, smiling. "Besides, I could use some support. I'm kind of nervous. Actually, I'm a lot nervous."

"You don't look it."

"Seriously?" he said, brightening a little. "I don't usually stand up and talk in front of lots of people, so I'm worried about that. Plus, I rewrote some of the speech. And I'm not sure where I'll use the posters." He took a few gulps of the cool air. "I may use our fake sheep brain, except Fletcher might get too close and see that it's marshmallows." He took a few more gulps. "I should never have gone through with this. It's going to be a disaster." Two more gulps. "I think I'm going to be sick."

As they reached the top of the hill, a white Pontiac GTO with a cracked windshield and spots of ochre-colored rust pulled up beside them, music pounding, and continued to move slowly along the shoulder of the road. The car kept pace with Zak and Mia, then jerked ahead with a slight screech of tires and stopped. Kevin Rourke jumped out of the driver's door, came around the front of the car, and leaned against the front fender.

"Mia. Hey. Let's us get away from here," Kevin shouted into the wind.

Mia looked at Zak, then turned to Kevin Rourke.

"Sorry, Kevin," she said. "We're going to work on a project."

"With this loser? This…zero?" Kevin said it like "Z-row."

"Z's my friend, Kevin," she said. "I've told you that."

"I thought you were joking," Kevin said maliciously.

Mia shook her head.

"I like him. He's nice," she said, sounding like she meant it.

"Sure," Kevin said, snickering and digging his fingers into his hair.

"I'll see you some other time, Kevin," she said, looking away and walking so fast that Zak had to jog to keep up. Zak looked back and saw Kevin Rourke following them.

"Hey," Kevin shouted. "Let me give you a ride." He gestured back to his car.

"I'm fine," Mia said loudly. Then she stopped, glanced at Zak, then back at Kevin, who had caught up with them.

"Let's get away and go get something to eat," Kevin said, reaching out for Mia and touching her sleeve. She pulled back her arm quickly as if Kevin Rourke's touch was fire.

"Look, stop chasing me," Mia said firmly. She tore off the maroon and white letter jacket and held it out in front of her. "Take it. I've been meaning to give it back."

Kevin knocked the jacket out of her hand so it fell in a heap on the sidewalk.

"What's this all about?" Kevin asked challengingly.

"No more games," she said. "I need to do what's right for me."

"Listen…," Kevin began, bending down and picking up his jacket and brushing it off. He looked at Zak out of the corner of his eye. Zak saw confusion, distrust, frustration, and anger, which made Zak tense his muscles. Zak thought about self defense moves he'd seen on TV: lightning-fast karate kicks and kidney punches. Zak didn't like his odds. Running away was always an option, but he couldn't leave Mia. That wouldn't be right. Besides, he knew he couldn't outrun Kevin Rourke. Stop, drop, and roll? No, that was for fires.

"You need to listen," Mia said. "I'm tired of wearing your jacket and listening to you and your friends. The world doesn't revolve around you."

"You're making a mistake," Kevin said.

"The only mistake was taking your jacket in the first place," Mia said.

Zak was impressed with Mia and the way she handled herself. She refused to be bullied. But there was something more. It was like she'd made a decision that she'd been meaning to make for a long, long time.

"I'm sorry, Kevin," Mia said. "I hoped you were different. Better."

"Well, you're wrong," Kevin said.

Kevin's jaw tightened as he stared at Mia Holmes. Then his arm lashed out and shoved Zak in the chest. Zak was amazed that he was able to stay on his feet even as Kevin moved toward him and spit into his face.

"Kevin, don't!" Mia shouted.

"He's a zero," Kevin said, grinning. "Zero."

Zak stepped back a little and crouched low to protect himself. Kevin swung hard with his right fist, a powerful, practiced explosion. Zak had never been in a fight before, so as Kevin's arm came toward him, he tried to imagine what it would be like to get hit. The pain. The bruises. His teeth…he didn't want to lose any teeth. He didn't like the idea of blood, either.

Zak closed his eyes and shielded his head with his left arm.

The blow came hard, and knocked Zak onto his back. But a fraction of a second before that, he heard a loud crunch and a scream as Kevin's fingers crumpled from contact with the plaster cast. Kevin Rourke dropped to his knees onto the sidewalk, cradling his injured right hand.

Zak looked around, dazed, surprised, but unhurt. Mia helped Zak get to his feet and they took off running, occasionally looking back at Kevin crouching on the sidewalk.

"That was crazy," Zak said breathlessly, still shaking from the fight.

"You're a hero!" Mia shouted.

"I'm a dead man," Zak said as they ran away arm-in-arm laughing.

47

Supernova

Mr. Larkin drew a long black cross on the whiteboard at the front of the English classroom. In the top left quadrant he wrote the word "Civilization" and in the top right he wrote "Savagery." The clock showed three minutes until class was to begin.

Jeremiah Koll stopped at Zak's desk, casting a large, amorphous shadow that covered Zak, his desk, and most of Omar Tahir, who sat behind him. Jeremiah wore baggy jeans, a black T-shirt, and a letter jacket with "Jer" embroidered on the front. Zak looked up into Jeremiah's troubled face.

"Z," Jeremiah said, bending closer to Zak. "I heard something."

"Huh?" Zak asked uncertainly.

Jeremiah Koll always made Zak nervous. They'd been in classes all through middle school but hardly talked or acknowledged each other's existence. It was like they lived in parallel worlds. Jeremiah was an athlete. He played on the high school varsity football team in eighth grade as a starting offensive lineman and was the only ninth grader to letter in football in the last eight years. Zak...was Zak. Small, invisible, inconsequential.

Standing next to Jeremiah always made Zak feel smaller than he was, so he kept his distance. Now it seemed that their worlds were getting a little closer.

"I heard how you broke your arm climbing that tree," Jeremiah said. He touched Zak's cast with a large, muscular finger.

The rest of the class strolled into the classroom, looked at Jeremiah and Zak, and quickly sat in their seats. Everyone stared. This was something new and unusual, like an earthquake or an eclipse or a supernova. The room was still except for the squeak of Mr. Larkin's marker on the board.

"There was a rope that I tried to get down," Zak said.

"What's the deal?"

"Some kind of message," Zak said. "I don't know who did it."

"You think it was for Mr. Brown?"

Zak nodded slowly.

"That's not good," Jeremiah said.

"I talked to the principal and the police," Zak said. "At first they thought I did it. Now...I don't think they have a clue."

"We gotta do something," Jeremiah said.

"That's what I think," Zak said. "But I don't know what."

"Mr. Koll," Mr. Larkin said loudly from the front of the classroom. "Please take your seat. Class is about to begin."

"Things are happening," Jeremiah Koll said as he shuffled to his desk. "Things are definitely happening."

48

Satyagraha

Zak noticed a change in his history class. Students arrived on time and alert. Cell phones were tucked away in pockets and purses. Even Dez Mitchell wandered into class awake and with his eyes open.

"My question for today is: how did we win the Revolutionary War?" Darius Brown began.

"Superior firepower," Randy Caton said quickly.

"Actually, Mr. Caton, the British had the advantage in skilled troops, better weapons, and the finest navy in the world," Mr. Brown said. "America should never have happened. The odds were against it."

"Oh," Randy Caton said slowly. "My bad."

"Then how did we win?" Nicole Anderson asked.

"I believe that was my question, Miss Anderson."

"We live here," Jeremiah Koll said. "That had to count for something. And they're like 3,000 miles away with an ocean in between."

"Two good points, Mr. Koll," Mr. Brown said. "Home

field advantage, if you will, and the distance—which affects communication, supplies, decision-making, and more."

"The French," Mia Holmes said. "Didn't they come to help?"

"They did, Miss Holmes," Mr. Brown said. "The French were not fond of the British. In the early stages of the war, the French supplied the colonists with muskets, gunpowder, and even uniforms. After the Battle of Saratoga in 1777, the French formed an alliance and formally recognized the colonies. Their supplies of soldiers, artillery, and naval support were keys to winning the war."

"Did we fight better or smarter than the British?" Betty Ng asked.

"General Washington was a talented, inspiring leader. He studied British strategies and won some key battles. He and other colonial generals learned about the British style of fighting and made adjustments in every battle."

"What do you mean by 'British style of fighting'?" Trudy Taylor asked.

"War looked different back then," Mr. Brown said. "Imagine a large field with armies on two sides coming together. Thousands of men about three to five deep. Everybody on each side fires at the same time. If the armies get close to each other, the soldiers try to skewer each other with bayonets. Or pitchforks. Or club each other with sticks."

"Whoa," Jason Wiley said.

"At the time that was called 'conventional warfare,'" Mr. Brown said.

"What other kind of fighting is there?" Mia Holmes asked.

"Unconventional warfare," Mr. Brown said, smiling.

"I could have figured that one out," Martee Freeman said sarcastically.

"Unconventional warfare refers to activities such as spying, sabotage, and guerrilla warfare," Mr. Brown said.

"Gorilla warfare?" Moleman said, laughing. "Like at the zoo?"

Darius Brown went to the whiteboard and wrote "Guerrilla Warfare" in large letters.

"It's a different kind of animal, Mr. Mould," Mr. Brown said. "Guerrilla warfare is where you use small, independent forces to surprise, frustrate, and wear down an enemy. It's playing by different rules."

"Isn't that cheating?" Martee Freeman asked.

"It's war. It's about killing people," Randy Caton said.

"That's the idea, Mr. Caton," Mr. Brown said. "In the American Revolution, most of the guerrilla fighting was done in the South—North and South Carolina, Georgia, and Florida. It was carried out by men like Francis Marion, called the 'Swamp Fox,' and Andrew Pickens and Daniel Morgan."

"Swamp Fox?" Zak asked.

"Marion and his men would attack quickly and then disappear into the swamps. That's how he got the nickname. Another one of his strategies was to tell his men to aim for the officers. The officers had epaulets on their shoulders—fancy decorations—so they were easy to spot. If you kill the officers, there's nobody left to lead."

"So they won?" Martee Freeman asked.

"Not individual battles. That's not what guerilla warfare is about," Mr. Brown said. "In fact, Nathanael Greene and his army lost every battle with the British. Every one. But that wasn't the point. They wore them down. The British lost their appetite for fighting."

"It all seems so barbaric," Maggie Cho said.

"It is," Mr. Brown said. "Which is why you want to do everything you can to prevent war." He looked around the classroom. "Things have changed quite a bit since then. We now have aircraft, missiles, submarines, nuclear bombs, and tanks. However, the principles of conventional and unconventional warfare are fundamentally the same." Mr. Brown paused. "I should add that there is another kind of warfare."

"Peace?" Mia Holmes suggested.

Darius Brown looked at his watch and then back at the class.

"In a manner of speaking, Miss Holmes," Mr. Brown said. "Let's talk about Gandhi for a moment."

"Isn't he that bald guy with the diaper?" Tom Gleason said.

"Correct," Mr. Brown said. "Mohandas Gandhi was a famous political and spiritual leader in India and a champion of something called civil disobedience or peaceful resistance. Gandhi called it satyagraha."

"Sa-tya-what?" Jeremiah Koll asked.

"Satyagraha. It's a non-violent method of fighting," Mr. Brown said. "Mr. Gandhi used satyagraha in India to fight against the British. Against tyranny."

"The British again? Don't they get along with anybody?" Randy Caton asked.

"In the 1920s, Gandhi led protests and strikes and boycotts and fasts and marches," Mr. Brown said. "He fought British taxes. He led his country to freedom and independence from an oppressive government. Sound familiar?"

"Wasn't the Boston Tea Party kind of doing this Sa-tya thing?" Nick Draves asked.

"What do you think?" Mr. Brown asked.

"They weren't shooting at anybody," Nick Draves said. "They just threw tea into the water. That's non-violent."

213

"It is," Mr. Brown said. "So you can say that the colonists in the American Revolution used three types of warfare—conventional, unconventional, and non-violent."

"Satyagraha," Mia Holmes said.

"This takes us back to the question I asked at the beginning of class," Mr. Brown said. "Miss Anderson?"

"Yes?" Nicole Anderson responded, surprised.

"What was our question?" Mr. Brown asked.

"I can't remember that far back," Nicole Anderson said.

"Give it a try," Mr. Brown said.

"Um…how did we win?" she said uncertainly. Mr. Brown nodded. "Maybe you should ask Z. I mean, he probably knows."

"Mr. Dale. What do you think?" Mr. Brown asked Zak.

"I think we won using different ways of fighting. And fighting at home with an ocean between us, like what Jer said." Zak tilted his head, thinking. "But isn't it also how long they could wait? I mean, if you just want to win fast, you go with all your firepower. But if you have more time—like ten or twenty or a hundred years—you can wear the other side down with guerilla warfare or like what Gandhi did in India."

"Exactly," Mr. Brown said, nodding and rubbing his hands together. "Know your enemy—his strengths and weaknesses. And know your own strengths and weaknesses."

49

The Pencil

Mia met Zak at his locker. It was getting to be a habit…a habit Zak liked. Since Mia had returned Kevin Rourke's jacket, she was cut off from all the new people she'd met. None of them would talk to her. They would pass her in the halls and whisper or ignore her. That left her isolated, with only a few other friends from her classes. And Zak.

Zak emptied his locker and put books into his backpack.

"Hi," Zak said. "I'm writing out a list of the things I'll need for the presentation. I don't want to forget anything."

"What's that?" Mia asked, pointing to Zak's pencil. It was yellow, about two inches long with teeth marks and a black eraser worn down to the metal. "How can you use that little pencil?"

"I've had it since the start of school," Zak said. "I start with a new one on the first day and try to make it last all year."

"That's stupid," Mia said.

"I almost did it once in middle school," Zak said. "But I think this is the year."

"How can you even hold it? And there's no eraser."

215

"It works for me," he said.

"Let's see it," Mia said.

Mia snatched it from his hand.

"Hey!" Zak said, surprised.

"I'll trade you," she said.

Mia dug into her purse, rooted around, and pulled out a plastic pen, which she handed to Zak.

"Take this," she said.

"I don't know," Zak said. "I'm not really a pen person. It's too…permanent."

"Nothing is permanent," Mia said. "You have to trust yourself, Z. Take risks. Be confident."

"I trusted that pencil," Zak said.

"It's holding you back, Z. Trust me."

He looked closely at the pen. The shaft was black with some white lettering and the image of a light bulb. He looked closer.

"AAA Lighting Company?"

"I don't know where I got it," Mia said. "Consider it a present."

"Thanks. I like expensive gifts like this."

"It's the thought."

"So what about my pencil?"

"I'll give it back."

"When?"

"When it's time," Mia said.

50

Final Day

"This will be my last day teaching history at John Quincy Adams Senior High School," Darius Brown said.

The classroom was quiet.

"What?" Jeremiah Koll said finally. "What are you talking about?"

"Your teacher, Ms. Jackson, is returning, which means I have reached the end of my term," Darius Brown said. "The contract was quite specific. As was Principal Decker."

"What are you going to do?" Mia Holmes asked. "What are *we* going to do?"

"I will finish up the year teaching at South High School," he said. "I was officially on sabbatical. Their final day is a week later than yours."

"A week later? Glad I'm not going there," Bruce Fetzlof said.

"We'll miss you," Katie Ramerez said.

"We actually learned something in this class," Jeremiah Koll said.

"Thank you for that," Darius Brown said, bowing. "I have

enjoyed teaching this class in particular. There are some marvelous historians among this group."

"I don't think it's fair," Trudy Taylor said. "To us."

"In honor of my last day as your teacher I have prepared a final examination," Darius Brown announced.

"What?" Nicole Anderson said.

"I…we didn't study!" Jason Wiley said.

"You didn't tell us there was going to be a test today," Martee Freeman said.

"Calm down, calm down," Darius Brown said. "If you've been paying attention in class you won't have any problems. It's only a few questions."

"I still think it's unfair," Candice Daniels said. "I mean, first you throw away Ms. Jackson's test and now this."

Darius Brown passed out a single blank sheet of paper to each student. He stopped at Zak's desk, his eyes on the broken arm.

"Do you need help, Mr. Dale?"

Zak raised his broken arm. "That's okay. I'm right handed, and my handwriting is actually better now."

Zak heard Mia's laugh from across the room. He figured this was a good time to try out his new pen.

"That's good to hear," Darius Brown said.

The teacher worked his way around the classroom, encouraging students to put away their textbooks, notebooks, music devices, and phones. When he was done, he straightened his necktie, cleared his throat, and rubbed his hands together.

"First, write your name clearly at the top of the page." He paused. "Now, for the first question, I'd like you to write the topic for this unit."

Maggie Cho raised her hand.

"Yes, Miss Cho."

"Can you tell us how many points each one is worth?"

"Very good. Thank you," he said. "I will let you know the value of each question as we proceed. Writing your name is worth one point. And the correct answer to the first question is also worth one point."

"What was the question again?" Randy Caton asked.

"The question is: what is the topic of this unit?"

Zak scribbled "American Revolution" with the new pen.

"Now write down the name of the country we were at war with during this conflict," Darius Brown said. "One point."

Zak wrote "Great Britain." He was surprised at how confident he had become. He had never felt prepared for a test. Even if he knew an answer, he was never sure it was right. Mr. Brown had made the class interesting and made him care about history. He and most everybody else actually listened—and remembered.

"Next, on three separate lines, write the three important dates we talked about and why they are important. Each of these has a value of five points."

"Can you give us a hint?" Fuzz Preston asked.

"Yes," Darius Brown said. "They were all in the eighteenth century. The seventeen hundreds."

"Thanks," Fuzz Preston said, shaking his head.

Zak had never taken notes in Mr. Brown's class, but he had listened to the discussion and read the textbook. A good part of that stuck with him. He wrote: "1776. The year the Declaration of Independence was written, printed, and signed. It was the document that told the British Parliament and King George the Third that we weren't going to put up with all the acts and taxes and that America was its own country, free and independent. It was signed by lots of people who risked their lives for an idea, which was America. If they lost they would be hanged to death.

Instead, they are now famous patriots."

He thought about the second date. He wasn't sure he had it right. "1783. (I think.)," he wrote, and continued, "That was the year the Treaty of Paris was signed, which was the end of the war. America really was independent."

The last date was also a bit iffy in his mind. "1789. The year George Washington was elected the first president of the United States of America. George was a general in the American army. He is also known as the father of our country. We never had much of a chance to learn about George."

Thirteen years seemed like such a long time to go from saying you want to be independent and really being independent. A lot of people died during that time. They believed that being separate and free was important enough to risk their lives. That was real courage. It's what soldiers did all the time. They risked their lives.

"Is everyone ready to move on?" Darius Brown asked.

"Just a second," Trudy Taylor said as she chewed on her lower lip and quickly wrote another a sentence. "Sorry. Okay. Thanks."

Darius Brown bowed briefly to Trudy Taylor and then cleared his throat. "Write the names of five important figures in the American Revolution," he said. "One point each."

Zak wrote James Madison, Benjamin Franklin, Thomas Paine, John Adams, and George Washington. Then he added Thomas Jefferson and Alexander Hamilton. As he looked at the names he felt he knew something about every one of them. It was a good feeling.

"Now, name the person who led his country to freedom from British rule through non-violent fighting. In the 1900s."

Zak wrote Gandhi on the sheet. He couldn't remember how to spell Gandhi's first name.

"Our next question is worth ten points...or one. Depending

on your answer."

"Or nothing if you don't know it," said Fuzz Preston.

"That's up to you, Mr. Preston," Darius Brown said. "The question is this: what is the name of Abraham Lincoln's wife?"

Heads shot up around the classroom.

"Hey...," Moleman shouted out.

"You told us...," Betty Ng said.

"That is the question," Darius Brown interrupted, circling his desk at the front of the class. "What is the name of Abraham Lincoln's wife?"

Zak heard swearing, confusion—and then laughter. Deep, reckless, uninhibited laughter. Jeremiah Koll's large body rocked forward and then back. Zak had a perfect view of the big man moving like an earthquake in front of him.

"I don't get it," Nicole Anderson said.

"Then...you...ain't...been...listening," Jeremiah Koll said, wiping a laugh tear from his eye and struggling to control himself.

Zak couldn't help but laugh along with Jeremiah.

Zak looked at the paper in front of him and then up at the face of Mary Todd Lincoln. Who was she? The wife of a famous president. An ordinary person. Was it fair to say that she was a nobody? If so, he was a nobody and everybody in class was a nobody. Still, every one of them was part of something larger that connected them together. They were all part of history and America. America was made up of a lot of nobodies.

Zak bent over his paper, wrote "Nobody," and added an exclamation point.

"The final question is an essay question," Mr. Brown said. "It is in two parts and worth a total of fifty points, so take your time."

"Fifty?" Dez Mitchell said.

"The question is as follows," Darius Brown said. He went

221

to the whiteboard and wrote quickly, then turned, pointed to the words he had written, and said, "Who are you? And who do you want to be?"

51

X

Zak walked through the hallway concentrating on his next class. English. He didn't know what to think about *Lord of the Flies*. What would he do if he were stranded on an island? What would anybody do? He looked at his Batman T-shirt. What would Batman do? Is there a devil within us who keeps dragging us down or an angel who tries to lift us up? Maybe there are no devils or angels. Maybe we're all on our own. He didn't know the answer.

As Zak walked along, he noticed the people ahead of him slowing. The two with letter jackets in front took short, shuffling steps. One of them was over six feet tall and the other was a little bit bigger. Zak couldn't see over them. When he tried to make a jog to the left to get past them, another letter jacketed body cut him off. He tried to turn around but that escape route was blocked off by a red-haired person in a letter jacket. Zak was being guided into a corridor and suddenly forced to stop. He was trapped. Alone.

"Hey," Zak said. He was sweating. He recognized a couple of them. Football and basketball players. "What's going on?"

"Talk. We need to talk," said the six-foot two-inch football player with dark hair. His jacket identified him as "Jack."

"I don't…," Zak began. He was feeling small. He was surrounded by three of them, and the other appeared to be acting as a lookout, standing apart and keeping everyone else away.

"And you need to listen," said the shortest of them who poked a finger at Zak. His name or nickname was "Bud."

Zak had seen them before. The red-headed one ran into him in the hall.

"You need to stay out of other people's business," Jack said.

"Yeah," said the third jacket whose name was "Ted."

"Look, I don't…," Zak said.

"Didn't I tell you to shut up, little man?" Jack said, leaning in toward him, and holding the shoulder of his broken left arm.

Zak nodded. His arm throbbed.

"We've had enough of you," Jack said.

Jack grabbed Zak's good arm and twisted it behind his back. Then pulled up. Zak screamed but a hand quickly muffled the sound. He bit hard on the hand. A second later he was lifted and slammed against the cinder block wall. His left side this time. His broken arm felt numb. His eye hurt where his head struck the wall.

"Keep it down," a voice cautioned in a hoarse whisper.

"Look at you in your Batman pajamas. Think you're some kind of superhero?"

"We know what you done and who you talked to," Bud said. "And whose side you're on."

"It's as simple as this," Jack said, spreading out his hands. "There's a price you gotta pay."

"Huh?" Zak asked uncertainly, close to tears. "A price for what?"

"Hold his arm," Jack said.

Bud grabbed Zak's right arm and held it against the wall. The

224

pale, hairless forearm looked almost the same color as the wall.

"Hold him down. Hold him down."

Zak watched as Jack brought out a big black marker and drew a large "X" on the underside of his right arm.

"'X' marks the spot," Jack said.

"It's gonna happen. Tomorrow. You just don't know when."

"Snap," Jack said. "Snap, snap, snap."

Bud pushed Zak so he stumbled backwards and landed on the floor in the corner with his head against the cinder block.

"We'll be waiting."

Zak took a deep breath and watched silently as they left. The last one, the lookout, the one who said nothing, turned to look back at him and smiled. Kevin.

52

Nothing

Zak shut the door as quietly as he could and tried to sneak into his house. Larry came up to sniff Zak's leg. Zak ignored him.

"Zak? Is that you?"

Zak didn't answer. He headed for his room.

Mrs. Dale's head appeared around the corner, then the rest of her.

"Your sister has a game tonight." She paused and looked closer at Zak's face. "What happened?"

Zak tried to push past, but Mrs. Dale held her ground. She lifted the hair away from his eye.

"What happened?" she repeated.

"Nothing."

Zak kept his head down.

"Zak. What happened to your eye?"

"I told you, nothing."

"Were you in a fight or something? Is it that teacher again?"

"No. I'm fine. I just…just let me go to my room. Please?"

"If you're involved in fighting, we have to deal with this."

"I just want to be left alone, okay?"

Zak walked wearily to his room and closed the door.

53

Courage

Zak was shaking. He had been sitting on his bed staring at the floor for three hours. He didn't want to eat. He didn't want to watch TV. His presentation was tomorrow…in front of the entire ninth grade class. But he wasn't sure he was going to show up. He looked at the "X" on his arm. It felt like it was eating through his skin.

There was a soft knock on his door.

"Go away," he said.

"Can I come in?" a faint voice said.

Zak walked to the door and opened it a crack.

"Mia?" Zak said, surprised.

"Are you okay?" she asked. "I talked to some people…and I got worried. When you didn't answer your phone I decided to come over."

"I'm not feeling too good."

"Your eye," she said, concerned. It was still swollen and the cut was starting to scab over.

Zak turned around and picked up dirty clothes from his floor and bed and tossed them into his closet. Mia walked into the room and closed the door behind her.

"I really don't want to talk about it," Zak said.

Mia picked up a stack of comic books from the desk chair and sat down. She stared at Zak.

"You were there for me," she said. "That meant a lot. I thought maybe you'd want to talk."

"Yeah, well, this is different."

Zak rolled back his sleeve to show the "X" on his forearm. He'd tried to wash it off. He'd scoured his skin and nearly burned himself with hot water, but it was unchanged. A jet-black "X" about three inches by three inches. Another variable.

"What? Who did that?"

"A bunch of goons. Including your friend Kevin. Jumped me in the hallway before English class."

"In school?"

Zak nodded. He still didn't look Mia in the eyes.

"They said they'd break my arm tomorrow."

"That doesn't make sense. Why?"

"I don't know," Zak said. "I don't know if it's this business with Mr. Brown or you or something else."

"Me?"

"I've never been in this position. I mean, I...nobody knows me...like I said before, I'm invisible...then I start hanging around you and climbing trees and breaking my arm and getting punched by Kevin and talking to the police and I don't know what's going on." He thought for a moment. "I just want things back the way they were."

"Do you really mean that?" Mia asked.

Zak kept rubbing the mark on his arm as if hoping it would disappear. It just made his arm redder.

"All I know is that I used to not matter," Zak said, shaking his head back and forth. "And now that's changed."

"Z, you do matter. That's a good thing."

"Right now I just want to quit," he said, and then added, "I'm not going to school tomorrow."

"You can't do that."

"Yeah? Watch me."

"You can't." She paused. "That's…what I did," Mia said quietly.

Zak lifted his head and looked at Mia.

"What are you talking about?"

"In my last school," she said. "Somebody thought it would be funny to make up a story. About me. About…an abortion."

"That's not funny."

"I told them to stop. That just made it worse. Everybody talked about it, it was on the internet," she said. "It wasn't true. Everybody knew it wasn't true."

"You can't let that stuff get to you," Zak said.

"I thought I could count on my friends," Mia said. "Turns out…I didn't have any."

"I don't believe that."

Mia was crying.

"I was popular. But it's…not…the…same…as…having… friends."

"Someone must have believed you," Zak said.

Zak waited for Mia to stop crying.

"My friends didn't say anything. It was terrible. There was nobody. Nobody."

"Your parents…," Zak said.

"It's not the same."

"I'm sorry, Mia."

"Th…thanks," she said, wiping her eyes on the sleeve of her white blouse. "I look back…I didn't believe in myself. I didn't stand up. And I didn't have any friends. So I just…quit. It was easy."

"You can't quit school."

"My dad was transferring. We were waiting for the end of the school year. So I came here early."

The two sat in silence except for Mia's occasional sniffles.

"I'm sorry, Mia," Zak repeated.

"You can't quit, Z."

"But you did. You got to start over."

"It's not starting over," she said. "I feel like I'm still running. I don't know who to trust. And I don't know who I am. Do you know what I'm saying?"

"Mia," Zak said. "You can count on me."

"But…I don't know if you can count on me. Don't you see?"

Zak thought about that for a second.

"You're here, aren't you? You're here looking out for me."

"But…"

"That's what friends do," Zak said.

Mia sat thinking. "What I'm saying is that you can't give up," she said.

"They said they'll break my arm. My other arm."

"Break your arm?"

"I have to be there for my presentation," Zak said slowly. "But I'm…afraid."

"You can go to the police…or the principal."

Zak shook his head.

"Would you?" He looked at Mia. "The police can't do anything. It's not a crime to put an 'X' on somebody's arm. And what's the principal going to do? Expel everyone?"

"But if you give up…," she began.

"They win? I'm fine with that. Winning…it doesn't matter. I don't care about winning."

"That's not what I was going to say," Mia said more forcefully than before. "If you give up…you lose. You lose. That's not the same as them winning. You have to live with that forever." She crossed the room, knelt down, and touched the mark on Zak's arm. "You can't lose."

Zak felt the touch of Mia's fingers tracing the lines of the X as if it were some kind of blessing. "And if I get beat up? If they break my arm?"

"You don't lose."

His mind was blank.

"I don't know."

"I can't tell you what to do. I'm the last person to listen to," Mia said.

"I'm not strong enough."

"Sometimes courage is just asking for help."

"I wouldn't know where to go."

"Z," Mia said, "you're not alone."

54

The Conversation

Zak slept through the night but woke tired, weak, and afraid. He still wasn't sure what he would do—or even what he *should* do. If he went to school he knew there was a good chance he'd get beaten up. And if he didn't…he'd live in fear for the rest of high school.

Zak closed his eyes, took a deep breath, and let the air out slowly. He thought about praying but decided on action instead. He put on his dress clothes and took one last look at the dark "X" on his arm before trying to button the sleeve. Fear was a thing. You could walk around it, you could touch it, you could smell it. He knew that. It was part of him.

Zak grabbed his backpack, the folder with his presentation, and the display boards that Mia had helped him with, and walked slowly toward his front door.

"I'm going to school," he said to no one.

"Have a good day, Zak," his mother shouted out.

"Yeah," Zak said weakly.

Zak bent down and touched Larry on the head.

"Wish me luck, Lar," he said.

Larry licked the back of Zak's hand and looked at him with sad eyes.

On the walk to school, Zak carried the display boards in his right hand. His head pounded as he crossed the street, stopped, and looked at the school from a distance. It was an ordinary red brick building surrounded by trees. He looked at the Adams Oak near the entrance. It stood solidly as it had for decades, as it would continue to do no matter what happened that day.

Zak stopped again about 100 feet from the school entrance and breathed in and out to try to calm himself. The face of the building stared back at him. He felt like two hearts were beating in his chest.

He walked calmly through the doors, past the chattering crowds, and down the hallway. A few steps later Zak could see a big black "X" on the door of his locker. He stared at it a long time, not daring to touch it, not putting down his backpack or posters.

Then he heard a familiar voice.

"Did we get the right one?" it said.

"It's the one with the three eights. I know it's right. I watched him open it," another voice said.

Zak turned around slowly and saw three shapes crowding around him.

"We're surprised you even came," Jack said, sneering.

"Not as much of a chicken as we thought," Kevin said. He shoved Zak toward the locker.

"Stupider than a chicken," Bud said.

Right then, for the first time that day, Zak relaxed. He wasn't afraid. Over the past 12 hours he had imagined himself beaten and broken and bloody. But here...everything was real, not exaggerated. Not like in the movies or comic books or his imagination.

"Scared?" Kevin said, smiling maliciously, pushing his face into Zak's face.

Zak set down the presentation boards, took off his backpack, and pulled back his right shirt sleeve to reveal the "X." Then he held out his arm.

"Here," Zak said.

"What?" Jack said.

"Break it," Zak said. He was calm. At ease. Breathing slowly.

"What…you think it's that easy? That it'll all go away?"

Zak continued to hold out his arm.

"When we're ready," Bud said.

"Yeah," Kevin said. "Let you sweat."

Zak then heard another voice. Familiar. Big.

"What's up?" the voice said.

It was Jeremiah Koll.

The three turned slightly and Zak could see Jeremiah's round face framed between Jack and Kevin's heads.

"Koll," Bud said, gesturing with a quick jerk of his head. "This is a private conversation."

"I won't tell nobody," Jeremiah said. "I can keep a secret."

"Get lost, Koll," Jack said.

"Okay," Jeremiah said. "But I need to show you something first."

"Make it fast," Jack said, looking from side to side.

Jeremiah took a step toward Jack.

"Here, hold these," he said, handing Jack his notebook and history textbook. Jeremiah took off his letter jacket and handed it to Bud. Jeremiah was again wearing a black T-shirt with a small pocket on the left side. It was stretched tight and showed his bulk and his muscles.

"We ain't your personal slaves, Koll," Bud said, grinning at his friends and snapping his gum.

"Hurry up about it," Kevin said. "We're busy talking with our friend Mr. Z."

Jeremiah stretched out his right arm and turned it slowly to show his forearm. A big "X" stared back at them. Zak looked at the mark. He didn't know what to think. What was it doing there? Who put it there? What did it mean?

"What?" Kevin said.

"What's that for?" Jack said.

"You tell me," Jeremiah said.

"We got no argument with you, Koll," Jack said.

"Looks like me and Z got matching arms," Jeremiah said. He looked at Z and nodded. "Matches the locker, too."

"Just clear out, okay?" Jack said.

"What about Z?" Jeremiah said.

"He's on his own," Bud said.

"We got a conversation," Kevin said.

"Uh-uh," Jeremiah said.

"Look, we were just having a pleasant discussion with our friend," Jack said.

"Batman was going to show us his super powers," Kevin said.

"He don't need no super powers," Jeremiah said. "He's got friends."

Jeremiah raised his right arm.

Zak turned and saw most of his history class converging on the locker and holding out their forearms. Each one had a big "X" on it. Some in red marker, some in blue, and some in black. Moleman was there, and Bruce Fetzlof, Nicole Anderson, Betty Ng, Martee Freeman, Tom Gleason, Candice Daniels, Fuzz Preston, Randy Caton, and Jason Wiley. Even Trudy Taylor proudly held out her arm. And Mia. Twelve of them.

Zak had to fight back tears.

"You okay, Z?" Mia asked, showing him the green "X" on her arm.

"Thanks," he said, not able to say much more.

"Thank Betty," Mia said. "She got the word out. A regular Thomas Paine."

Zak turned to look at Betty. She gave him a fierce smile.

"Nobody cares about a couple of freshmen," Jack said.

"More than a couple, I'd say," Jeremiah said.

"We didn't do nothing," Bud said.

"Neither did we...yet," Jeremiah said. He turned to Zak. "You want to use my marker, Z?" Jeremiah held out a large black permanent marker.

Zak looked at Jack's arm. Then at Jack's face. For an instant he thought about branding the boy's forehead with a big "Z." He'd be like Tyrone Power. Zorro. He could see it in his mind. But that wasn't real. He didn't want to be hated or feared. He just wanted it to be over.

"He's already got a mark," Zak said calmly. "Inside."

Jeremiah moved slightly to the side, opening up a space for Jack, Bud, and Kevin to pass through. They took off quickly and as they did, everybody started talking and congratulating each other and comparing Xs and laughing.

"You okay, Z?" Mia asked, moving closer to Zak.

Zak nodded.

"What were you thinking?" she asked.

"I thought I'd try that Gandhi thing," Zak said nonchalantly.

"Gandhi was assassinated," Mia said. "Did you think about that?"

"I guess I didn't read that far in the history book," Zak said.

55

Showtime

Zak sat in a chair on the auditorium stage and looked at the students and teachers finding their way to their seats. He was still euphoric from the show of support from his history class. He smiled as he remembered Jeremiah and the twelve arms with Xs raised to support him. It filled him with confidence.

Zak looked down at the purple cast on his left arm and read the words Mia had written: Defender of Justice. It was a challenge. His friends had defended him when he needed it most and now it was up to him to defend others.

The chairs on the stage were arranged in a semi-circle surrounding a wooden podium with a microphone. Zak looked to either side of him. On his left sat Jocelyn Vrek and Ted Crady, and on his right sat Eric Randall and Kim Sather. Eric Randall held a giant papier-mâché tooth, which went along with his speech called "New Frontiers in Dentistry." Kim Sather flipped through a stack of note cards and had her easel and visual aids behind her chair. Zak didn't remember much about Kim Sather's presentation on single cell organisms. Jocelyn Vrek was doing something on

238

genetics and Ted Crady's presentation was about robots. Zak wondered about his own speech. Then he thought about Miles. Zak was sure that Miles' presentation was better than any of these, including his own.

Dr. Fletcher went up the side steps, walked to the podium, and leaned toward the microphone.

"Testing? Testing?" he said. His voice boomed over the speakers. Satisfied, he turned toward the presenters, who looked up at him with strained, hollow smiles.

"A few minutes everyone?" he said. "When we are ready to begin, I will make the necessary introductions and you will deliver your presentations? Am I right?"

"Yes, Dr. Fletcher," Zak said. Ted and Jocelyn looked nervous. Eric opened his mouth but didn't say anything. Kim Sather said, "I'm looking forward to it, Dr. Fletcher."

"Good? Everybody?"

Dr. Fletcher clapped his hands together and began to walk away.

"Dr. Fletcher? Dr. Fletcher?" Zak said suddenly. "Can I have someone help me with my visual aids? Because of my arm, I mean?"

Zak lifted his broken arm and made a pained expression with his face so he would appear as weak and pitiful as possible. He nearly hit Jocelyn Vrek on the head.

"Mr. Dale? Under the circumstances I think that would be perfectly fine. But don't expect the sympathy vote? We will evaluate the content, the depth of your science. Yes?"

"Yes?" Zak said, nodding. "Oh, and about that summer job...?" he added quietly.

"Still waiting for a sign," Dr. Fletcher said quickly.

Dr. Fletcher wandered off in the direction of the booth and the lighting controls.

Zak used his head to gesture to Mia. She walked up the side stairs.

"All clear," Zak said. "I got the go-ahead from Fletcher."

Mia pulled up a chair just behind Zak and sat down.

"I told you. You have nothing to worry about," Mia whispered.

"My visual aids!" he said in a panic, looking around frantically.

"Relax. They're in back. I got them earlier. Dr. Fletcher let me take whatever I wanted. Including Felix."

"Felix? The armadillo?"

Mia nodded.

"What am I going to do with that? There's nothing about armadillos in my speech."

"Make something up," Mia said. "I told Fletcher that it had something to do with new research on the brain. Just add something about that."

"Armadillos?"

"You'll do fine," she said.

Mia smiled and walked to the back of the stage, returning with a box that included the five new posters, the sheep brain jar, Felix the armadillo, a plastic brain model, and several things Zak didn't recognize. She set the box in front of Zak and sat down.

Kim Sather gave him a quizzical look. "What's with the armadillo?" she asked.

"Um…new brain research," Zak said. "Amazing stuff."

"Oh," Kim Sather said uncertainly.

Zak looked out at the auditorium seats. It was now a place of noise and motion. People talked and hugged and moved around. It was like a giant living creature, changing and shifting.

Zak scanned the seats to see if he could spot Miles. Miles said he would try to sneak in to see the speech—and to bug Fletcher.

Dr. Fletcher walked down the side aisle, up the stairs, and to the podium. The audience lights dimmed.

"Your seats? Take your seats, please?" Dr. Fletcher began. He waited for fifteen seconds and then scanned the auditorium.

"Thank you for coming," he said. "I am Dr. Cyrus B. Fletcher and today is the first in what I hope will be a long history of what I am calling the John Quincy Adams Science Series. I am proud to be joined today by three other science professionals. I would like to introduce Dr. Matt Sampson from the Department of Veterinary Medicine at Wellspring College." Applause. "Dr. Henrietta Williams, D.D.S., of the Williams Dental Clinic." Applause. "And Dr. Alec Fisher from the Miller College of Dentistry." Applause. "The four of us will act as judges to determine who will be the inaugural winner of the John Quincy Adams Science Series Prize, a $100 scholarship donated by...Wonder Burger." He squinted at his notes, scowled, and added, "'A mighty fine burger.'"

"Seems like a lot of dentist judges," Mia said quietly. "You going to be able to work with that?"

"Huh? Oh, I don't know," Zak said distractedly. He had reached into his pocket to turn off his phone. He didn't want that to go off during his speech. "I wasn't paying attention."

Zak was zoning out. He looked at Felix, who stared back at him. Zak was nervous about getting up and talking in front of his entire grade. He rubbed the "X" under his sleeve.

"We will begin with Ms. Sather," Dr. Fletcher said.

Kim Sather got up, arranged her easel and visual aids, and began to talk about microorganisms. As before, Zak had meant to listen, but as soon as he heard the terms "building blocks of the universe" and "cellular structure," his mind made a quick detour. Who was he? What did he want to be? He wanted life to be fair. But what did that mean? Good people died. Tornados and hurricanes and floods and earthquakes destroyed homes. Ants got stepped on. None of that was fair. So why did he want to change the natural order of life? Why did he feel offended when life made things difficult? What about Job? He'd believed, but lost everything—his family, his possessions, and his health and dignity. God made things right for Job in the end…but tell that to his dead family.

Mia nudged him with her elbow.

"What?" Zak asked.

"Did you hear that?"

"What?"

"The part about microorganisms and dental plaque," Mia said.

"Missed it," Zak said.

"And about all the microorganisms in the mouth…more than 300 species," she said.

"Missed that, too."

"She's really hitting hard on this dental theme."

"Uh-huh."

"Are you nervous?" Mia asked.

"Sort of. Yeah," Zak said. "I'm feeling a bit sick, actually." He looked at her and managed a pained grin. His face was pale.

"You'll do great." Mia gave him an encouraging smile.

Zak couldn't concentrate on any of the speeches. Ted Crady was next. Robots could do amazing things—walk and talk and even play musical instruments. Maybe even robot dentistry. Zak turned to Mia and rolled his eyes. Jocelyn Vrek started talking about Gregor Mendel and peas, then jumped ahead to talk about genetic engineering and how it would soon be possible to "design" people—choose a baby with brown eyes and blonde hair. That part was a little scary, she said, but what about children who were cancer-free and had perfect white teeth that didn't get cavities? "In a few short years, we could make dentists and dentistry obsolete!"

she said excitedly. Zak looked at Dr. Fletcher. He seemed to frown at this, as did several of the other judges. Eric Randall was fourth with his presentation on "New Frontiers in Dentistry." He talked about implants and sensors inside the mouth, cell phone teeth, re-growing teeth, lasers, and teeth strengtheners. In his conclusion, Eric held up his tooth model and said, "One thing we do know about the future is that people will always have teeth. And whether they use lasers or robots or nanotechnology or"— he looked at Jocelyn Vrek—"genetic engineering, we will always need dentists." Zak looked at Dr. Fletcher and the judges again. They all had big smiles and vigorously applauded.

"What else do you have on teeth?" Mia asked quietly.

"I brushed my teeth this morning," Zak said. "At least I think I did."

"No, seriously," Mia said.

"Just that bit I had in there before," he said. "Except I took it out."

"Really?"

"It didn't seem to fit," Zak said. "You got anything better?"

"I did find out that nine-banded armadillos have about 30 teeth."

"What does that have to do with neurobiology?"

Zak didn't have time to wait for an answer. He stood and approached the podium as Mia set the posters on the easel and placed the jar with the brain, the brain model, and Felix on the table directly in front of the audience. Felix and his 30 armadillo teeth grinned at Zak.

Zak swallowed, looked toward Mia, and then scanned the audience. He gave a nod to Dr. Fletcher and a weak smile. Vomiting was a definite possibility.

He took a deep breath and looked at his paper.

"The human brain is an amazing machine," he began.

The speech was pretty much the one he had given earlier, except he had the advantage of Mia helping out. She added sizzle, and a lot more visuals than Zak had expected. When he said that the human brain was the size of a coconut, she brought out a coconut and held it next to Eric Randall's head. Everybody laughed. When he mentioned the Egyptians taking brains out through the nose, she acted that out using the head/brain model and Silly Putty. When he mentioned that part of Einstein's brain used to be in a jar floating in formaldehyde in Kansas, Mia held up the jar with the sheep brain, a photo of Einstein, and a map of Kansas. People seemed to be interested and enjoying themselves.

As he looked toward the back of the auditorium he saw one of the doors open. A shaggy-haired figure slipped inside and sat in the last row. Miles.

Zak silently cheered.

"The cerebrum makes up the largest part of the human brain. It is separated into a 'right brain' and a 'left brain.'"

Mia pulled the model of the brain into two parts, holding one in her right hand and the other in her left as Zak talked about Dr. Sperry's studies and famous right brain thinkers.

Zak looked at Fletcher, who was clearly enjoying his position as lead judge and founder of the John Quincy Adams Science Series. He'd said he was "waiting for a sign." Zak knew what that meant. He didn't feel strongly enough about Zak even after Zak had cleaned the science room, improved his grades, and earned his place among the final five presenters. It was just what Miles and Aurora had said. Fletcher would string Zak along and then give the job to Kim Sather. Right then Zak wanted to stick his finger up his nose and pull out a giant booger. He took a deep breath through his nostrils. Clear. Nothing there. Drat.

He kept going.

"Most people are left brain thinkers, but some studies have shown that most preschoolers start out as right brain thinkers. And that school changes us."

Miles should be giving his presentation right now, in this auditorium, with a chance to win the Wonder Burger scholarship, Zak thought.

Zak looked at the face of the armadillo. It stared at him. Judging him. Or was he judging himself? Suddenly the lights flickered. He looked over at Mia. Thin strands of her blonde hair stood out and hovered in the air from static electricity. She gave him a big smile and a nod. Zak felt a surge of energy, like the flip of a light switch, as if all the pieces of his life were somehow falling into place.

"Brain studies of animals are revealing as well," he continued.

He looked at Miles.

"Like…"

He looked at Fletcher.

"Like…," he stuttered.

He looked at Felix.

"Like…sheep," he said finally, determinedly, emphasizing the word "sheep."

Zak looked at Mia and gestured toward the jar with the sheep brain. He mouthed the word "Open" to Mia. She went over toward the jar. Zak's body was on fire.

"The brains of sheep," he said as Mia opened the jar. "Sheep brains." Mia held the jar out to the audience. "Sheep brains are… are…"

Zak reached over, dug his hand into the jar, and scooped out the "brain." He held up the dripping, soggy gray form and took a large bite.

"A delicacy in some cultures," he said, olive oil dripping down his chin.

"No!" a voice shouted. It was Fletcher. "Poison! It's poison!"

Fletcher and Principal Decker were both on their feet trying to get close to the stage.

Mia reached over and tore off a piece of the brain and put it into her mouth.

"Somebody stop them!" Decker shouted.

The audience was going crazy.

"Someone call 911!"

More than 300 cell phones instantly appeared in students' hands, lighting up the auditorium, all dialing 911 at the same time. It was like being at a rock concert.

Mia looked at Zak and laughed. She reached into her mouth and pulled out a coin.

"Penny for your thoughts?" she asked.

"Tastes like chicken—with lint," Zak said, chewing on the marshmallows and oil.

Zak and Mia stood on the stage while the crowd raged below them. In the back row of seats, Miles stood applauding. Off to the side Zak noticed Mr. Brown for the first time. When did he come in?

Zak looked down and saw Fletcher with a hand on his chest as several teachers tried to carry him away. Zak leaned into the microphone one last time before the principal reached the stage.

"Oh, armadillos have about 30 teeth. I forgot to mention that," he said. "And boogers. Boogers. That's for Miles."

56

Black History

Zak stood off to the side of the stage waiting for the paramedics and police to finish their work, for the ringing in his ears from the fire alarm to go away, and for Assistant Principal Petrovich to return and scream at him again. As he stood there, the foul taste of marshmallow and oil and lint in his mouth, Darius Brown approached him.

"Quite a performance, Mr. Dale," Mr. Brown said, smiling. "Most entertaining."

"I…I thought you were gone," Zak said.

Darius Brown nodded.

"I returned to see you and your presentation, Mr. Dale," he said.

"Really?" Zak was surprised. "Um, it's not what you think. I kind of self-destructed…on purpose. We had to give our speeches before, and Dr. Fletcher didn't like the one from my friend, even though it was really good. I couldn't let him down. My friend, I mean. It wasn't fair."

"I assume your grade was at risk as well?" Mr. Brown asked.

"And a summer job," Zak said dispiritedly. "I was up for this summer job in science. But it probably wasn't going to happen."

"That was a courageous thing to do," Mr. Brown said.

"Stupid is more like it," Zak said.

Zak didn't know what to say next. He looked up at his teacher's face. Something had been bothering him.

"I have a question," he said. "No offense or anything."

"Yes?"

"It's just...," Zak began, "the whole time you were here, you never mentioned any...minorities. Except when you said we weren't going to talk about Martin Luther King, Jr."

"That is correct."

"But why? There were blacks in the American Revolution. And the Civil War was a lot about slavery. And Gandhi was an inspiration to Martin Luther King, Jr. At least that's what it said in the textbook."

"Mr. Dale, I was hired to teach history," Mr. Brown said. "I have found that in an environment such as this—where there are few teachers or students or parents of my particular color—there is a risk of being labeled for what I look like rather than what I teach."

"So if you talk about blacks..."

"Some might say that I teach 'black' history and not 'real' history," Mr. Brown said. "The American Revolution is much less controversial."

"But you talked about people and choices and fighting for what you believe," Zak said. "That's...the same."

"There are parallels," Mr. Brown said, nodding. "Our founding fathers inspired a lot of people. A good observation."

"Thanks," Zak said. "Um...our class, we really miss you. We mostly sit and watch DVDs now."

"Thank you," Mr. Brown said. "Now I have a question."

"Okay," Zak said, curious.

"I have a teaching position available this summer, Mr. Dale. There is no pay involved. It is a true black history class. I would be honored if you would be one of my associates."

"For real?"

Mr. Brown nodded.

"I don't know anything about black history," Zak said quietly. "And I'm not black, in case you didn't notice."

"True, true," he said. "But you know about people, Mr. Dale. History is about people. Your perspective would be invaluable. I believe we would all learn a great deal."

"I…I think I'd like that," Zak said.

57

The Genius

Zak wandered away from school and toward…he didn't know what or where. A new world had opened up and he felt as though all his senses had been electrified. He listened to the chatter of squirrels in the trees, he felt the warmth of the sunlight deep into his muscles, he saw cars streaking past in slow motion, he smelled blooming spring flowers and cut grass, and he tasted…fake sheep brain. He definitely needed to brush his teeth. Looking up, he found himself at the end of Miles' driveway.

"That was genius," Miles shouted as he walked from his house to greet Zak.

"Thanks," Zak said, embarrassed, as Miles gave him a high five. "It was fun. But I probably didn't think it through all the way."

"It was perfect." Miles said. "Like Godzilla destroying Tokyo."

Right then—for the first time in his life—Zak felt that he and Miles were on the same level. Equals. Growing up he'd always considered himself inferior, admiring what his friend knew and could do, and knowing he could never match it or even come close. Zak now realized there were different kinds of intelligence, different talents and abilities.

"I knew I had to do something when I saw you come into the auditorium," Zak said.

"You didn't need to do anything, Z. It was my fight," Miles said. A few seconds later he added, "Besides, everything worked out."

"What do you mean?"

"That judge, that Watanabe guy? He called and talked to my mom about me taking some classes at Wentworth College next year. There's even a scholarship."

"Congrats," Zak said, feeling good for his friend. "You're going to college and I'm…getting kicked out of high school, probably. We make a great team."

"They can't kick you out for this," Miles said. After a brief pause he added, "Of course, you could get kicked out for that fight you were in and didn't call me about."

"Sorry," Zak said. "I didn't want both of us to get beat up."

"That's a good point," Miles said, nodding and grinning.

"What's amazing is that most of my history class was there," Zak said, looking into the sky and then back to Miles. "They just appeared. Jerry Koll, Mia, Moleman, even Trudy Taylor. I still can't believe it. It's like I matter or something."

"Don't sell yourself short," Miles said.

Zak smiled. Short was exactly what he didn't feel. For once he felt he was the right size.

"I have to go home and talk to my parents about what happened," Zak said, looking in the direction of his house. "They're not going to be happy."

"Oh. Your mom called looking for you," Miles said

apologetically. "I forgot to mention that."

Zak pulled out his phone. He'd forgotten to turn it back on after his speech.

"Z, the way I see it, when this is all over we're going to celebrate the best speeches that were never finished," Miles said quickly. "We're going to Wonder Burger."

58

Californium

Zak walked up the sidewalk to his house with a smile on his face. He'd survived. Not only that, he knew he had friends he could count on. Miles, of course. Mia. And his history class. People who didn't know his name a month ago had stood up for him. His presentation had gone...as well as expected. He'd landed a summer job. Even his broken arm didn't seem to itch. Zak opened the door, ready for anything.

"Zak? Is that you?" It was his mother's voice.

"Yeah," he said, setting his backpack on the floor where he knew he would get yelled at for it. He didn't care. Larry came over to greet him, wagging his pointy brown tail.

"Where have you been?" Mr. Dale asked. His face was unreadable. "We tried to call, but you didn't answer. We were worried."

Mr. and Mrs. Dale and Chloe came out into the living room.

"Really? Um...I was at school. Talking with Mr. Brown. And then with Miles," Zak said. "Why? What's up?"

Zak knew he was in trouble, but he wanted the good feeling to last as long as possible.

"We got a call, Zak," Mr. Dale said.

"From the police?" Zak said, grimacing.

Mr. Dale shook his head.

"From the school," Mr. Dale said.

"About some out-of-control science experiment," Mrs. Dale said.

Zak screwed up his face.

"Seems that your science teacher wants you expelled," Mr. Dale said.

"Tell us what's going on," Mrs. Dale said with a forced calm.

Zak thought about Fletcher, Mia, Miles, his history class, and everything that led up to that day.

"I kind of talked about this with Dad," Zak said.

Mrs. Dale turned her head quickly to look at her husband who gave her a "Don't ask me" expression, then turned back to Zak.

"It was my presentation. The one for science," Zak said.

"Go on," Mrs. Dale said.

"Dr. Fletcher got mad at Miles for doing a speech on boogers."

"Boogers?" Chloe said. "He gave a speech on boogers?"

"Don't get any ideas, young lady," Mr. Dale said.

"That's funny. Boogers," she said. "Boogers, boogers, boogers."

"I didn't feel right about giving my speech on the brain when Miles had all this research and charts and stuff, and didn't even get a chance to present. It was really good. Real science. Dr. Fletcher wasn't being fair."

"This is what we were talking about outside the other night," Mr. Dale said to Zak.

Zak nodded.

"And I told you to do what's right and what's in your heart,"

Mr. Dale said.

Zak nodded.

"And not to worry about the grade," Mr. Dale said.

Zak nodded.

"Where was I? Why didn't anybody talk to me about this?" Mrs. Dale said, frustrated.

"I didn't get talked to either," Chloe said.

"Shhhh," everyone said to Chloe.

"Why is everybody 'Shhhhing' me?" Chloe asked, plopping into a chair, folding her arms, and pouting.

"So what did you do?" Mrs. Dale asked.

"I didn't really do all that much," Zak said. "Not really."

"Teachers don't try to get their students expelled on a whim," Mrs. Dale said.

"I was giving my presentation, which is on the brain, and Mia was helping me."

"That girl who was here the other day?"

"Yeah," Zak said. "She was helping with visual aids because of my arm."

"Keep going," Mrs. Dale said.

"Do you remember when I cleaned up Dr. Fletcher's lab that one Saturday?"

"Yes," Mrs. Dale said. "Larry remembers it, too."

Larry was now lying on his side in a corner of the living room.

"I broke this jar with a sheep's brain in it and Mia and I cleaned it up and made a fake brain out of marshmallows and put it in olive oil in a jar so Dr. Fletcher wouldn't notice. Mia brought that jar as part of my presentation and I was talking and then I looked out and saw Miles sitting in the back. He wasn't supposed to be there, but he was watching. So I opened the jar and ate the brain. Mia ate some, too."

"Hold on. You ate the brain during your presentation?" Mr. Dale said, shaking his head.

"It wasn't real," Zak said.

"Marshmallows and olive oil?" Mrs. Dale said, laughing.

"Fletcher flipped," Zak said, smiling. "I suppose he thought we were going to die from formaldehyde poisoning. But it was just marshmallows."

"That was the end of your presentation?"

"Uh-huh," Zak said. "Dr. Fletcher had to be carried off on a stretcher. He was hyperventilating."

"Did they call for an ambulance?"

Zak nodded.

"What was everybody else doing?" Mr. Dale asked.

"I don't think they knew what was going on," Zak said. "Principal Decker stood up and got everybody out of there fast. I was the last speaker anyway."

"I can't imagine you can be expelled for this," Mrs. Dale said. "It's not like you did anything wrong."

"Inciting a riot? Abusing hazardous chemicals?" Mr. Dale said.

"It was marshmallows and olive oil, Dad!"

"I know, I know," Mr. Dale said. "I'm not saying I go along with any of that. We wanted to hear from you before we sat down with the principal and assistant principal—again." He paused. "We're getting to be good friends."

"Sorry," Zak said.

"I thought you were trying to get a job from Dr. Fletcher this summer," Mrs. Dale said. "This isn't going to help."

"I was," Zak said. "But it wasn't going to happen. Besides, Miles is more important."

"Maybe it's not as bad as we thought," Mr. Dale said to his

wife.

"Oh, I forgot," Zak said, brightening. "I actually got a job for the summer. It's teaching a summer class with Mr. Brown."

"Mr. Brown?"

"My history teacher. Or he was. Ms. Jackson's back now."

"So you'll be teaching? History?"

"Helping out," Zak said. "Black history, actually."

"Black history?" Mr. Dale asked. "What do you know about black history?"

"I think it's a lot like regular history. Except it fills in a lot of parts that get left out," Zak said. "Mr. Brown says it won't be a problem."

Zak stood looking from his mother to his father and back again.

"Congratulations, Zak," Mrs. Dale said. She hugged him.

"Of course, it doesn't pay anything," Zak said.

"We'll have to figure out how you can earn some extra money," Mr. Dale said.

"You think this Mr. Brown will take you even after this episode at the school?" Mrs. Dale asked.

"He was there," Zak said. "He saw it all."

"Unbelievable," Mr. Dale said, shaking his head.

Then Mrs. Dale's eyes opened wide.

"Oh!" she said. "We got a postcard from your grandmother."

"She's alive?" Mr. Dale said jokingly.

"Of course she's alive," Mrs. Dale said.

"I want to see it!" Chloe shouted. "I want to see the postcard."

Mrs. Dale handed a colorful card to Chloe. It had a picture of the Golden Gate Bridge and the words, "Greetings From...San Francisco."

"Is she okay?" Zak asked.

257

"She's in California," Mrs. Dale said.

"Go, Grandma!" Zak said.

"I can't read what this says," Chloe said, tilting the card on its side.

"Here," Zak said, holding out his hand.

"No," she said. "I want Dad to read it."

Mr. Dale reached down and took the card.

"It says, 'Hello, family! We are in San Francisco! We drove 3,000 miles so far! Miriam and I drove across the Golden Gate bridge and rode on a street car and went to a baseball game. I'm having the time of my life. Tomorrow…to the beach! Then down the highway to Mexico. Love to all. Grandma Gloria. XOXOXO.'"

"All these years and I don't understand my own mother," Mrs. Dale said.

Zak laughed.

"What's so funny?" Mr. Dale asked.

"She made it. She made it to California and the ocean like she wanted," he said. "It's one of the last things on the periodic table. Californium. Grandma's, like, in her element."

59

An Instant in Time

Zak stood on the steps of Mia Holmes' house with his right index finger inches away from the doorbell. In the glass of the storm door he could see the ghost that was his reflection, and in that hazy, distorted image he saw himself as more real than ever before. He stood straight, his face appeared older and more confident, the cast on his arm seemed to vanish; he was…more substantial. Zak smiled, pressed the doorbell, and listened to the chimes ring inside the house. The door opened and Mia appeared, dressed in jeans and a T-shirt, with a big smile on her face.

"That was, like, the greatest thing ever," she said excitedly, quickly joining Zak on the steps. "It was unreal."

"I still can't believe it," Zak said, shaking his head back and forth.

"What about the look on Fletcher's face?" Mia said, laughing. "I thought his eyes were going to pop out."

"I think he really thought we were going to poison ourselves," Zak said. "I heard he had to go to the hospital."

"I can still taste that stale marshmallow and olive oil. It's lucky we didn't get sick."

"It was pretty disgusting," Zak said.

"You want to come inside?" Mia asked.

"Um…I'd rather just walk around, if that's okay," Zak said. "It's a nice day."

"Sure," Mia said, pausing. "I'd like that. Except…I have to stay close. I'm kind of grounded."

They followed the walkway to the sidewalk and headed east toward a house under construction. A light, cooling wind mussed their hair. Robins darted around the newly-planted maple trees.

"Did you get a call?" Mia asked, the smile gone. "From school?"

"From the principal?" Zak nodded slowly and bit on his lip. "You too?"

"Yeah," Mia said, sighing. "My mom got a bit panicked."

"Same here. But I just told my parents what happened. They were okay with it, I think. They even congratulated me. I mean, it's not like we did anything wrong."

"Actually, if you think about it, it was pretty bad," Mia said. "Causing panic in the school and all those 911 calls for help."

"That wasn't exactly our fault," Zak said.

"The fire alarm going off and the paramedics, police, and fire department all there."

"I suppose."

"Having to shut the school for the rest of the day."

"Okay, okay," Zak said. "Still, it's not like anybody got hurt."

"That one kid twisted his ankle and Melissa Roberts chipped a tooth. And there were three that fainted, including the one judge. And the principal looked like he was ready to strangle you."

"I was just trying to explain what happened and he got all red in the face with all those veins popping out on his head," Zak said defensively.

"It'll be the end of the John Quincy Adams Science Series," she said. "And I don't suppose Wonder Burger is too happy, either."

"It does sound pretty bad," Zak said.

"What do you think will happen?" Mia asked after a long pause.

"About what?"

"About you," she said.

"Me?" Zak said, thinking. "I'll get an 'F' in Fletcher's science class. That's a no-brainer. The principal and assistant principal will probably try to get me some kind of counseling. I may even get suspended or expelled. Kevin and his friends will try to break my arms or legs or face when they get a chance, except they may be too scared of Jer, so that's up in the air. The school will send apology letters to all the parents and probably do some more disaster preparedness drills." He stopped and then added, "We should get a nice write-up in the paper, though. Could be front page."

"So, it kind of balances out," Mia said sarcastically.

"Yeah. Pretty much," Zak agreed. "You?"

"I'm already grounded, and my dad's going to kill me when he gets home. Maybe I should have him talk to your parents," she said. "I'll probably be in line for some counseling, too."

"Maybe we can do that together," Zak said hopefully.

"You seem to be dealing with this pretty well," Mia said. "I mean, this really blew up. Everybody knows who you are. You're not invisible. Aren't you going to miss that?"

"I don't know," Zak said. "It was nice having the world so small and nobody expecting anything from me—especially myself. But even with all the risks, I think I'll like this better. I

261

found out something I never knew."

"What's that?"

"There's people who care about me. Aside from my relatives, I mean," Zak said. "I can't believe you and Jer and everybody showing up like that. I never saw it coming. I was prepared to get beat up pretty bad."

"It's what Mr. Brown was talking about when he asked, 'Who are you?' and 'Who do you want to be?'" Mia said. "All of us, we found out the answer. We want to be the good guys."

"I didn't think being a good guy would be so hard," Zak said. Mia searched through her purse as Zak talked. "What are you looking for?"

"I have something for you," she said, taking out a small object.

Mia handed Zak the stub of a pencil. Zak's pencil.

"Thanks. But I don't need it," Zak said. "I got used to that pen you gave me. You keep it."

"What am I going to do with it?" Mia asked.

"Something to remember me by," Zak said.

"I don't think I'll have any trouble remembering you. Not after today."

They walked along a little farther, circling back toward Mia's house. Suddenly Mia started laughing.

"What's so funny?" Zak asked.

"I just realized it's prom night," Mia said. "I forgot about that. I remember once thinking how important it was."

Zak and Mia looked at each other, then Zak glanced down at the sidewalk. Next to the grass in one cracked section of the concrete, hundreds of tiny brown ants swarmed around an anthill like a single organism. Mia watched with a quizzical look as Zak stopped and knelt down to examine the activity more closely. All the ants were working together, helping each other, with a single purpose. Zak imagined long dark ant tunnels underneath his feet and spreading out across the city. Being an ant couldn't be easy, Zak thought. Ants had to deal with rain and cold and kids messing up their homes and animals eating them for lunch. They were all nobodies. Still, they had each other. That meant a lot.

Zak stood, brushed his jeans, and looked into Mia's eyes.

"Do you want to *not* go to prom with me?" he asked.

"I'd like that," Mia said.

Zak held Mia's hand for the first time and they walked back toward her home. It was a beautiful day. The sun lit up the blue sky, the aspen leaves quivered, the smell of hyacinths hung in the air, and Zak knew that in that one instant—a single moment in the billions of years of the cosmos—he was the happiest man alive.

www.ingramcontent.com/pod-product-compliance
Lightning Source LLC
Chambersburg PA
CBHW050722180626
46814CB00002B/567